A truck exploded

An orange and black ball of fire roared upward, spraying out chunks of fenders and bumpers, lethal pellets of glass and metal, trunk lids and hoods. The attackers were caught in an inferno of shrapnel and flame.

Track slammed his last 30-round stick up the magazine well of his M-16 and started forward. George and Desiree were flanking him. Ahead of them, the enemy, their bodies burning, fired their subguns wildly. Behind, the civilian defenders stood awestruck at the horror.

Track knew that he, Desiree and George were doing the work that needed doing— the killing!

**Now available in the exciting new series
from Gold Eagle Books**

by Jerry Ahern

TRACK

The D.E.A.T.H. Hunters

JERRY AHERN

A GOLD EAGLE BOOK FROM
WORLDWIDE

TORONTO · NEW YORK · LONDON · PARIS
AMSTERDAM · STOCKHOLM · HAMBURG
ATHENS · MILAN · TOKYO · SYDNEY

First edition October 1985

ISBN 0-373-62009-8

For Trapper—a real-life pro and one heck of a nice guy.
To you and "Mrs. Trapper," all the best.

Printed in Canada

1

Sir Abner Chesterton rolled over the side of the rubber
Avon inflatable and into the surf, keeping the muzzle of
the Walther MPK subgun high and out of the spray.
With one hand he wrenched at the grommeted rope rail,
glancing to his left, feeling the change in the weight of
the craft as Zulu dropped off on the other side. Together they drew the craft over the breakers and shore-
ward; Chesterton's legs were soaked through the jungle-
pattern camouflage fatigue pants, and spray pelted his
face as he strained against the force of a wave sweeping
against his legs. He asked himself, as he did more often
these days, if he was getting too old for running around
in stocking caps, cammie makeup, battle gear and fin-
gerless cloth gloves playing commando? But as usual in
those moments of self-doubt, there wasn't the time to
consider an answer and so he just went on.

"Here, Sir Abner," Zulu's voice shouted over the
roar of the waves.

"Right," Chesterton replied. He tugged at the reluc-
tant craft once more and it lurched onto the sand.

Chesterton sagged to his knees beside it, bringing the
Walther subgun up to chest level in a guard position.
Zulu was moving again, dragging the rubber boat across
the sand and up onto the rocks beyond. Chesterton's
eyes swept the beach. That there were guards who pa-
trolled here was an indisputable fact—whether or not

they had already covered this particular section of beach was all that remained in question. But he saw nothing.

He pushed himself up, running in a low crouch toward the rocks into which Zulu and the gray Avon inflatable had disappeared.

He jumped an inconveniently placed hummock of black igneous rock and zigzagged into shelter, where he flattened himself against the rock face and waited. Then he heard Zulu again. "Sir Abner—here!"

"Right." Chesterton nodded into the night and started back deeper into the rocks. He could barely discern Zulu in the darkness, but saw the giant black African in time to avoid crashing into him. Chesterton dropped into a crouch beside him, the MPK still in a high port. "Looks as though we made it."

"Yes, it does at that. Shall we?"

"Right," and Chesterton snatched his day pack from the interior of the Avon inflatable. Zulu had already lashed his pack into position. Chesterton looked back along the rocky maze and toward the dark sand of the beach once more—no one in sight. He slung the MPK again, then nudged it back from beneath his right arm and out of the way. "At the count of three?"

"If you like," Zulu answered.

"One, two, three!" And Chesterton raised from his crouch into a standing position, Zulu doing the same, both lifting the starboard side of the inflatable as well, shoving the boat back against the rocks, letting it lean down. It sagged slightly.

"Should be safe enough here. And if we get discovered, we won't need the craft anyway," Zulu said.

"That's right, just cheer me up, Zulu. Bloody decent of you."

The Oxford-trained voice echoed with laughter from the darkness. "So terribly glad I'm amusing you, Sir Abner." And then Zulu was off, working forward into the rocks and landward, Chesterton running behind him.

Chesterton had checked the face of his Rolex Sea-Dweller when he'd shouldered his OD day pack, and he looked at it again as they emerged from a chimney of rock. Ten minutes had elapsed. Zulu descended the pile of rocks, skidding along on his rear end into the shadow. Chesterton followed, but suddenly he was skidding faster than he had planned, faster than he could control, and he splayed his hands and arms and legs, slowing himself.

And then he was dropping and he drew up his knees, his feet taking the impact, then his ankles. He rolled with it in the darkness, coming out on his feet in a crouch. The MPK that he had strapped across his chest before climbing up through the chimney was in hand again.

"Zulu?"

"Ahead of you, Sir Abner."

Chesterton nodded to the darkness. He could already smell the jungle, and he pushed himself up and trotted forward, picking his way over what felt like the surfaced roots of large trees. The roots formed a web-like obstacle course as he moved ahead. His eyes were as accustomed to the dim light from the stars and the quarter moon as they would ever be, and all he could discern were shadows.

He was brought up sharply, slamming against Zulu. "Sorry, old chap."

"There should be guards along that trail ahead and below us," Zulu whispered. Chesterton felt Zulu's breath against his right ear.

"What trail?" Chesterton whispered back.

"I was raised in the jungles of the Congo, Sir Abner—there is a trail."

"If you say so, dear boy. Do we wait for the guards and take them out?"

"I think that would be best," Zulu whispered back. "Come," and Zulu was moving again, but slowly, and Chesterton followed his friend's lead, the 9mm subgun in an assault position clutched in his right fist, tensioned against its taped web sling. His left arm defended his face against the brushings of broad, dank-smelling, slippery-feeling leaves, his left hand swatting at the occasional mosquito. The repellent he had used was working, mercifully.

Zulu stopped, and Chesterton came up behind him.

He could make out Zulu in silhouette as Zulu turned toward him. "I hear the footsteps of at least two men," Zulu whispered. "One seems substantially shorter than the other."

"Regrettable you can't be more specific," Chesterton whispered back.

Zulu said nothing for a moment, then, "Yes…it is only two. You should perhaps take the shorter fellow—the stride of the other sounds quite long."

"You're serious, aren't you?"

"Of course, Sir Abner. Am I ever otherwise?" Then Zulu touched his hand to Chesterton's mouth to signal silence.

He could hear movement now, as well.

Zulu held a commando knife close to his face, and Chesterton nodded, reaching for the butt of his Gerber MkII fighting knife. Slowly, carefully, he worked loose the snap, extracting the black cat's-paw-handled blade from the black leather.

Chesterton edged forward slightly, realizing that he wasn't breathing. He corrected that.

One of the two men was speaking. "Fuckin' broad tells me, hey—you didn't pay for no blow job. And she starts puttin' her clothes on."

"Shit."

"I slapped her up side the head and told her, look bitch—you get ready to start combing—"

Zulu moved. Chesterton moved. The man who'd been talking shouted "Hell! What the—"

But Chesterton was too busy to catch the rest. The shorter of the two men was less than three feet from him now. Chesterton's left hand was moving, slamming against the rising muzzle of the assault rifle and hammering it away, his right arm arcing forward and his knife piercing flesh. There was a hiss, then the smell of bad breath and alcohol, and Chesterton fell on the man, wrenching the knife blade clear and then thrusting forward and down, into the throat.

Another smell of bad breath and the body beneath him ceased to move. It wasn't the neatest sentry removal he had ever done, Chesterton reflected, but not the sloppiest, either. That had been a few miles up from what later became Omaha Beach.

Chesterton looked up. Zulu was already standing. Chesterton grinned, still straddling the dead man. "I see what you meant. This fellow was a bit short."

Zulu didn't reply. He was already dragging a body back toward the rising ground that led into the jungle.

Chesterton wiped the blade of his knife clean against the trouser legs of the short one, then sheathed it. He caught the man by the heels and started to drag him along.

THEY MOVED MORE SLOWLY through the jungle after killing the two sentries; the very fact the men had been where they were proved that the intelligence Zulu had gathered concerning the place had been accurate—at least so far. And they could not strike at the heart of the island until dawn.

They stopped along the trail, two hours into the journey and two-thirds of the way there as best Chesterton could judge. Huddled in a clump of low brush beside Zulu, Chesterton asked the question that had been burning at him since the planning of the commando raid against Calico Island had begun. "What if this Mulliner person won't talk, just won't talk at all, Zulu?"

"I will loosen his tongue, Sir Abner."

"Assuming as much, I still ask the question. Mulliner may not talk no matter what you do to him. There are such men, you know. Men who can withstand drugs, hypnosis—all of it. Men who can withstand torture, as well."

"Then we are back to square one in our search for the ever-popular Colonel Hudson. Mulliner served three tours of duty in Southeast Asia with Stone Hudson. Hudson at one time was co-owner of Mulliner's establishment here. Likely Mulliner supplies Hudson with personnel from time to time. If Mulliner is not aware of Hudson's affiliation with the Master of D.E.A.T.H., he must have at the very least some means of contacting the good colonel. And that we must learn."

"And what if we cannot?"

"Then all of this will have been for naught, and we will kill Mulliner at any event since the world would likely be better off without him. Agreed?" Zulu turned in the darkness, and Chesterton saw the whiteness of Zulu's teeth and eyes.

"Agreed," Chesterton answered emotionlessly. Mulliner was, despite a rather brilliant war record in the jungles of Southeast Asia, currently the proprietor of a rather exclusive mercenary training center. Chesterton had known mercenaries, good and bad. But the men Mulliner trained were unique. Unlike the classic American or British mercenary, these men specialized in ter-

ror and death. They were not soldiers, but butchers.
"Agreed," Chesterton said again.

THE PAST HOUR HAD BEEN EASIER, the sky graying to
the east and the traveling through the jungle terrain
easier for it. The terrain itself was thinning as they
climbed up from the denser lowlands, the air cooler, the
mosquitos less bothersome. He could see Zulu clearly
now as they moved along, the fatigues the huge man
wore ringed and lined with the blackness of sweat,
making a pattern within the jungle pattern of the cloth.
Across Zulu's back was an AKM that would be left behind regardless of the outcome of the morning, to la-
bel the assault against the island mercenaries as Com-
munist inspired. At Zulu's right hip was a full-flap
leather holster housing a Browning Hi-Power. On the
left hip rode a massive leather pouch carrying four 13-
round magazines for the Browning. Beside the pouch
was an ornate Gerber fighting knife with a brass double-
quillon guard and butt cap, and a handle of rosewood.

In Zulu's hands was a stockless Remington 870 riot
shotgun.

They marched on.

It was thirsty work, and several times Chesterton had
tapped from his canteen. As they broke from jungle
cover into the rocks, Chesterton signaled Zulu to stop.
Chesterton pointed to his crotch and then to the rocks.
The African nodded.

Chesterton started off at a tangent, looking for a
suitable spot. Unzipping his fly, he started to do what
he had to do. And then he heard the voices. He stopped
himself, standing there, exercising willpower against the
forces of nature, not daring to make a sound.

"What's your watch say, Ernie?" said one of the
voices.

"Ten minutes yet before the relief comes. Relax, huh?"

"Shit, I hate guard duty."

Chesterton stood perfectly still. The voices were from directly below him and had he urinated across the rock as he had planned he would have urinated on one or both of the speakers.

He looked back over his shoulder for Zulu, but Zulu was nowhere in sight.

Chesterton held his breath, squinting. He'd had to have a leak for the last mile and only stopped when he'd felt he could go no farther. He opened his eyes and looked up. On the rocks opposite the small depression before which he stood, he saw Zulu. The African's face was lit with a rare grin. Chesterton grinned back, then raised the middle finger of his right hand in what had become the universal version of the transethnic, transnational salute. Everything was getting Americanized, Chesterton reflected.

Zulu pointed to his wristwatch and gestured as if to say, "A moment, please."

Chesterton shook his head violently.

Zulu nodded deliberately. In his left hand Zulu held a long tube of bamboo. In his right hand was something identical to it. Chesterton watched as Zulu attached one tube to the other—it was a blowgun, Chesterton suddenly realized. He watched as Zulu inserted a dart into the end of the blowgun. It looked as though Zulu held a second dart in the fingers of his right hand as he raised the blowgun to his mouth.

Chesterton looked down at himself and shook his head. He sighed. He did what he had to do.

"What the hell! That's—fer Ch—"

There was a low whistling sound followed by a gasp of pain. "Hey!" shouted a startled second voice. Chesterton looked up. Zulu's head nodded once and he heard the whistling sound again, then a muted, "Dammit! You—"

Chesterton zipped up and edged forward to peer over the rocks. Both men lay motionless beneath him. He looked across the rocks at Zulu. Zulu was calmly dismantling the blowgun. Chesterton started down from the rocks.

THEY MET NO OTHER GUARDS as they moved through the jungle. Chesterton glanced at his watch—two minutes remained before the new sentries would arrive and find the bodies of the two Zulu had killed with the poison-tipped darts. But relief details were always late, he told himself—this one would be, too. They had perhaps as much as five minutes—but inevitably the alarm would be sounded.

Zulu raised his left hand to signal a halt, then dropped to his knees. Chesterton followed his movements.

Zulu slipped right and with Zulu's bulk aside, Chesterton could see through the foliage to the plateau about a hundred yards above. It was nearly dawn and they had reached the far side of Calico Island. Cliffs dropped off beyond the plateau, Chesterton knew, leading to the sea. They had reached the school of John Mulliner.

Chesterton let out a long whistling breath. He glanced at his watch. At any moment, the sentries would be discovered. The alarm would be raised. Any chance of making an escape through the jungle back to their boat would be lost. If something went wrong and the aircraft did not arrive, they would simply die.

It was a sobering thing to consider, Chesterton thought.

Zulu was signaling toward the plateau, and Chesterton nodded. They had rehearsed this portion of the mission at least a dozen times in the three days they had

had to prepare. And they had elected to go it alone rather than having Dan Track return prematurely from his much-needed rest with Desiree Goth. If they had told Track of the mission, Track would have come, of that Chesterton was certain. Which was why they had told Track nothing.

Zulu signaled again, but Chesterton was already moving, the Walther MPK subgun in his fists. Sometimes, he knew, a man was at his best when the veneer of civilization was scratched away, as it was now. He kept running, taking the rise in longer, more even strides than he had thought he could, his breathing fine, his legs responding as if forty years had not passed since his first commando raid during World War II.

He glanced to his right—Zulu was beside him.

Not ahead of him.

Chesterton took the rise, bending his body into it, jumping the last yard or so. He was on the plateau now.

A group of buildings lay before him.

Smoke rose from one of them, probably the cook shed.

He'd memorized the camp's layout from the aerial maps Zulu had had done. He'd run it out foot for foot in the desert where they had trained for the mission, at a higher altitude than here so that here it would be physically easier. And now he ran to the building at the far side of the plateau where only Mulliner slept, the one building with air-conditioning and its own generator.

He saw the man before he heard him, running from a building beside the cook shack, and Chesterton swung the muzzle of the MPK toward him. The man shouted, "Somebody killed Ernie and—" Chesterton drew back the bolt, then squeezed the trigger, firing, not hearing the rest of the words over the rattle of the MPK and the boom of Zulu's shotgun.

Chesterton ran on, his heart pounding in his chest.

Ahead of him, he could see the building with its portable generator and air-conditioning unit.

The door opened and a woman stepped out.

The woman screamed when she saw him, and Chesterton fired into the dirt a few yards in front of her feet. Instead of running back into the building, she ran into the plateau's parade ground.

He could hear gunfire now from his right, and he swung the MPK in that direction, his eyes seeking out a target. He found three and fired at men with M-16s running toward him. One man spun and went down. The second and third were firing, and Chesterton could hear the boom of Zulu's 870, and the roar of a heavy-caliber assault rifle. Chesterton glanced over his shoulder. Zulu held his shotgun in his right fist and the AKM in his left.

Chesterton was nearly at the open door of the corrugated metal building; the girl was screaming from somewhere in the distance, and he remembered suddenly that she'd been wearing panties and nothing else. He smiled—he must be getting old, he thought.

Chesterton flattened himself against the doorframe and stabbed the MPK through the opening. He didn't want to kill John Mulliner—yet.

The MPK was nearly empty, and he reached for the Browning Hi-Power in the Special Weapons fabric tanker-style shoulder rig. He dropped the MPK on its sling and snapped back the Browning's slide, throwing himself through the open doorway into the darkness.

"Freeze your ass, motherfucker," a voice shouted from the darkness. Chesterton rolled and fired, a double tap, then another and another, into the darkness.

Gunfire ripped into the wooden floor near his head.

He was up on his feet, throwing himself into the darkness, his shins striking against something.

"Damn," Chesterton snarled, skidding on his knees beside some sort of low chest of drawers.

A burst of subgun fire ripped through the darkness, and the top of the dresser disintegrated.

Chesterton upped the safety on the Browning, holstering it across his chest, and raised the MPK. He fired high, trying not to kill, at least not yet.

The MPK was empty. The bolt locked and Chesterton dropped the magazine and rammed another stick up the well. "Mulliner! You haven't got a bloody chance, man. Throw out your weapon!" Chesterton shouted.

"Eat it!" a man yelled, and more subgun fire filled the room. Chesterton tucked back against the wall—he was losing time. He glanced at his watch. In five or six minutes the helicopter would be coming in and he and Zulu would have to be aboard it or dead.

"Mulliner! We don't want you—we want to find Stone Hudson."

Mulliner's reply was another burst of subgun fire. Chesterton's mind raced—he had counted shots, and the total was near thirty. If Mulliner had been caught unawares he would have snatched up the subgun but had probably forgotten any spare magazines.

Chesterton took the chance. He fired the MPK's entire magazine into the darkness over and to right and left of where he made John Mulliner's position.

A burst of subgun fire answered him, then another.

The subgun stopped in midburst. "Shit!" he heard snarled from the darkness.

Chesterton was up and running, the MPK at his side empty on its sling. The Browning in his right fist had half a magazine left. If it wasn't enough he would be dead.

He stormed into the darkness at the far side of the room.

He felt something tear at his left arm before he heard the sound. He didn't stop, throwing himself toward the muzzle-flash and down, rolling. He found form, substance—a human shape. He hammered the pistol into the darkness, feeling movement, hearing a groan and muted curse.

His left fist smashed out and he felt bone. Chesterton moved the muzzle of the Hi-Power against the face he could not see. "Move and you're bloody dead, Mulliner!"

"I won't tell you shit, man!"

"Where can I find Hudson? There's a man outside who would torture you for it. But I'll kill you before that. Or I'll let you live. Your choice, Mulliner. And if you lie, I'll be back and you'll die—I swear it."

He had never heard such conviction in his own voice. And now he heard the voice that belonged to the face he could not see. "All I know is he needed four guys with subarctic operations experience, and I got him the guys."

Chesterton relaxed the pressure on the pistol. He knew as he did it that it was a mistake. He felt the knife blade in the darkness, burning against the left side of his rib cage, then a coldness as he pulled the trigger of the Hi-Power again and again and again. He staggered back, his left hand touching his side and coming away wet. Something had splashed against his face, and he could taste a mixture that he knew was blood and flesh and maybe human brain matter.

He forced himself to his feet, lurching toward the doorway, the sick feeling in his stomach coming partially from the wound, partially from what he had done.

A figure filled the doorway, and Zulu's voice echoed across the darkness. "You learned what we needed."

It was a statement. But Chesterton responded as though it was a question. "Yes. Hudson needed four men with subarctic experience. It means he's going after Dan and Desiree in Idaho. It must be the reason. He slashed me along the rib cage." Chesterton sagged forward.

As Zulu caught him, Chesterton shook his head to clear it.

"I'm all right now," Chesterton said, throwing himself into a run. In the distance he could see the black shape of the helicopter.

He heard the roar of Zulu's shotgun again, then again and again. Chesterton fired the Browning, then stabbed it back into the holster. The AKM came flying toward him as he glanced back at Zulu, and Chesterton caught it and fired, lacing a 3-round burst into the chest of one of the late John Mulliner's mercenaries. Then half running, half lurching, he made his way toward the center of the compound. He heard the roar of the shotgun again and again. Chesterton dropped to his knees at the center of the compound, the assault rifle at waist level, firing 3-round bursts, cutting men down as they ran from the buildings where they had slept.

The AKM was empty, and Zulu's right hand flashed to his hip and the Hi-Power came into it.

Chesterton stabbed his right hand under his fatigue shirt, ripping open the buttons, finding the butt of the stainless PPK/S. The pistol was stuffed into his trouser band, the butt sticky with his own blood. He stabbed the pistol outward, his right thumb working up the safety. He fired once, then once more, then a double tap and another of the Mulliner mercenaries went down.

The rotor noise of the helicopter was almost deafeningly loud now. Chesterton threw down the AKM, firing out the PPK/S into three attackers. Two went down, one of the two still firing. Chesterton dived toward that man. The PPK/S was still in his fist, and he crashed it down against the bridge of the man's nose again and again. Chesterton rolled off him, half expecting the third man to cut him down. He looked up and saw that Zulu had the man's head drawn back by the hair, the blade of the African's knife slashing across the merc's neck. Chesterton averted his eyes as blood sprayed toward him from the severed artery.

Chesterton picked up the M-16 belonging to the man he'd just beaten to death, and started pumping the trigger, aiming the rifle toward the men still coming from the huts. To his left he could hear, half see Zulu with a second M-16, firing. Chesterton felt the sand pelt at his face, felt the downdraft tear at his clothes, and ran for the helicopter. He caught sight of Zulu as the huge African was swinging the butt of the M-16 at the head of an opponent. As stock and head met, the head snapped back, the nose gushed blood and the stock broke in half.

Zulu threw down the rifle and ran. As Chesterton reached the helicopter, the pilot was firing through one of the storm windows.

Chesterton launched himself up and through the door, rolling.

Locked in by spring clips beside the bulkhead were two M-16s, and Chesterton grabbed at one of them, working back the bolt, letting it fly forward, firing through the doorway. He raised the rifle as Zulu vaulted into the chopper.

Chesterton snapped the muzzle of the M-16 down again, firing 3-round bursts.

Over the roar of the rotor blades and the cacophony of gunfire he could hear Zulu shouting, "Take her up, man!"

And then Zulu was beside him in the doorway, firing the second M-16.

Chesterton could feel hot brass pelting at his flesh, worming its way down inside his half-opened fatigue shirt, burning at him. He kept firing down into the parade ground, running men everywhere.

He caught sight for an instant of the girl who had come from Mulliner's building—she still wore nothing but panties.

Chesterton sagged back, his assault rifle empty. The coolness of the air from the downdraft was making him shiver as the sweat dried on him. He grabbed onto a support strap with his right hand, lest the helicopter make a radical change in direction and he be pitched outward.

On his knees, opening Chesterton's shirt, then starting to examine the wound, was Zulu. Chesterton shook his head—the slash across his ribs hurt very badly. "This tanker holster you were wearing probably saved your life, deflecting the knife. I'm afraid the holster is damaged beyond repair, however."

"Aagh," he groaned, sucking in his breath against the pain as Zulu began to clean the wound.

Zulu said nothing. Chesterton wanted a cigarette very badly. As if Zulu had read his mind, the African opened Chesterton's cigarette case and removed a cancer stick. He put the butt between Chesterton's lips and stroked the lighter. "How people can smoke is thoroughly beyond me," Zulu remarked.

"I'm glad to hear you say that. It's a filthy habit." Chesterton inhaled the smoke deeper into his lungs than he could ever remember having done before.

It was good to be alive.

Now the task was to contact Desiree Goth and Dan Track at the mountain retreat in Idaho, and to keep them alive, as well.

2

Sergei Baslovitch was breathless. He stood staring up along the ski run, watching for Tatiana as she caught up. She was young and tireless on the slopes. He was not all that terribly far removed from being young, but well removed from being tireless. She was a natural on skis, and he envied her that. His mastery of skiing was technique and practice, hers was almost intuitive, but he was still faster. Yet she had never skied before they had come here under their new identities, and she was learning so quickly that by the end of the next season she would be faster, as well.

She was coming fast, trying for speed she couldn't yet control. "Sergei!" She screamed his name, laughing as he propelled himself laterally to intercept her, dropping his poles, catching her around the waist, both of them crashing into the snow. "That wasn't very graceful, Sergei."

"And you are not supposed to call me Sergei, Louise," Baslovitch said, using the name she had in her new identity. He was Peter Kroehler from Germany and she was his wife, Louise. Her German was as perfect as his. The part about being his wife was true—after the business in Mexico had ended, they had been married. Chesterton stepped in for Tatiana's absent father and gave the bride away, Desiree was the maid of honor, and Track was Baslovitch's best man.

With Desiree's underworld contacts and Chesterton's help, their new identities had been established as naturalized American citizens with perfectly forged documents as proof to anyone who was interested. Through Track's contacts, he had had Immigration and Naturalization Service records altered to match the forgeries, in exchange for Baslovitch spending twelve hours with the CIA's Special Section for Soviet Affairs. Baslovitch had not compromised his integrity, nor Soviet military security. He had spoken only about the structure of the KGB, an organization he had come to regard as the antithesis of the ideals of communism. In those twelve hours he estimated he had set back Soviet intelligence irreparably—at least this was what he hoped.

The real Peter Kroehler had been a West German police official of substantial personal wealth. It was the perfect identity change—Kroehler had no family, had died in a remote area of Austria, bizarrely enough as the result of a skiing accident. And Kroehler matched Baslovitch's approximate height and weight. Kroehler's identity was perfect because the German's personal wealth allowed Baslovitch to use the monies he had accrued over the years and spend normally. And Kroehler's background in police work let Baslovitch remain faithful to the tenor if not the substance of his own past.

Baslovitch had grown a beard, which he kept neatly trimmed, surprised by the amount of gray there was in it. His only two regrets at the identity change were his gun and Tatiana's hair. Kroehler had begun professional life in the German army's CID—and until his dying day carried Walthers. To aid in the deception, Baslovitch had parted with his P-7 and switched to a Walther P-5. Kroehler had not had a wife, so Tatiana's identity as a new bride was an understandable and supportable one. But Tatiana's golden hair would have been too obvious should some stray encounter bring them close to the KGB. So her hair was now dyed to a very pleasing auburn color that went well with her skin and her pale blue eyes. But still he missed her blond hair.

She was breathless in his arms from the long run down the mountainside from their house above the small Idaho ranching town of Storm City. The cold was bitter, the wind chill. But they had been housebound too long because of the record snowfall. After another, shorter, run there would be the warmth of the café and the lunch he had promised her. Later, he would get Andy Mistral or his son Morgan to drive them back up the mountain in the Sno-Cat. Baslovitch had taught Morgan Mistral how to use a handgun better and more effectively since first making the young man's acquaintance when buying groceries at his father's store. Mistral had lost his right trigger finger in an accident and never mastered handgun use with his left hand. With patience, Baslovitch had taught the boy not only to shoot well with his left hand, but to utilize the second finger of his right hand and to shoot right-handed again, as well. The friendship with the boy had been important to Baslovitch, because the other feature of the identity change that was very difficult was that under no circumstances could he or Tatiana risk contact with Dan Track, Desiree Goth, George Beegh, Zulu or Abner Chesterton. And they had become closer friends in the months spent fighting the KGB in Russia than Baslovitch had ever thought possible.

He realized he was still holding Tatiana very tightly against him. "What is it, Sergei?"

"Peter—remember?"

"Well—" she smiled, touching her gloved hand to his face "—I don't really want to be called Louise."

"How about Louie—hmm?"

"Louie? All right."

"Okay, Louie, let's get to town before we freeze. Race you again," and he laughed. She kissed him lightly once on the lips and he dug in his poles and was off. He looked back and she was right behind him.

If it had only hurt when he laughed, it would not have troubled him. Because there was nothing to laugh about. But it hurt when he moved the wrong way as he had when reaching for the telephone. It was the Consortium office in Los Angeles. "Chesterton here."

"Sir Abner? This is Bart Cook."

"Yes, Bart. Good talking to you again. Have you got anything for me?"

"Checked our contacts in Seattle and with a man we sometimes use in Boise—independent insurance agent who saw a lot of combat experience in Vietnam. Nice guy. But nothing on either end. If this Hudson guy and a pack of killers are infiltrating Twisted Oak, Idaho—where the hell is Twisted Oak, Sir Abner?"

"Off the south fork of the Salmon River."

"Then they're not based out of anyplace we can find. Maybe they air-dropped. People still do that, don't they?"

"Yes, Bart, people still do that. If you hear anything, contact me as quickly as possible."

"I'll keep my feelers out, Sir Abner."

"Quite—ringing off," and Chesterton cradled the receiver. The door opened into the office he had expropriated in the Miami headquarters for the Consortium, and Zulu, his cammies replaced by a consummately tailored gray three-piece suit, entered.

"Is there any word, Sir Abner?"

"No, no trace of Hudson or anyone like him heading into Twisted Oak. How about your and Desiree's contacts?"

Zulu perched on the edge of the desk while Chesterton adjusted his position. It was the bandaging that hurt, at least that's what he told himself. "Desiree has some very good friends in Seattle," Zulu began. "But they have detected nothing. They are still making inquiries."

"It has to be George then."

"And myself."

"That entire area is snowed in. No surface transportation in or out and the nearest airport where any runway could conceivably be cleared is a hundred miles away."

"I'll drop in, HALO it if I can."

"Right—we'll drop in."

"But your rib cage, Sir Abner—"

"I'm having this bandage changed in an hour—the doctor's coming up here. We can get started on the arrangements." Chesterton toyed with the yellow pencil resting on the green blotter of his desk. "Should I contact George, do you think?"

"The telephone company could give you no indication when service would be restored in the Twisted Oak area?"

"No, they put it down to storm damage. But it might be our friend Hudson. They have miles and miles of line and all one needs to do to suspend communications to a remote area like Twisted Oak is to sever the line in one spot. It could take days under these conditions for men in snowmobiles to find the one spot. They can pinpoint it within a certain grid, but it's not like a city telephone system. I can contact George in Butte, Montana. He could probably get in faster, leave go of this chain of mysterious deaths I've had him looking into along the Montana-Idaho border.''

"But you don't want to,'' Zulu said softly.

"I don't think Dan would want me to. When I told Dan that George was coming back to work for the Consortium, he was worried. Close calls for George, Ellen's paralysis. If this were to get George killed...''

"Leave George out of it. Let him do his detective work. Did you check the Butte area for any signs of Hudson?''

Zulu was lighting a pipe, and Chesterton watched the smoke curl upward. "Yes—without alerting George. Nothing there, either. But with the money available to Hudson through the Master, Hudson could have flown out of New York City to air-drop in Idaho for all we know.''

"I have always disliked coincidence, Sir Abner,'' Zulu said through a cloud of smoke. The tobacco was mildly aromatic and very pleasant, Chesterton thought absently. "Yet a coincidence is forming. A bizarre one.''

Chesterton nodded. "George investigating a chain of mysterious accidental deaths near the Idaho border. Desiree and Dan snowbound and inaccessible. And now we'll be going in.''

"I am a disbeliever in fate, but it is as if fate was drawing us to one specific spot.''

Chesterton shook his head, a shiver running along his spine. "Don't say that sort of thing, Zulu. Don't even think it.''

"We shall see. If you will arrange for the aircraft,'' Zulu said as he stood, "then I will arrange for the equipment and any additional weapons that might be needed.''

"Bring your electric socks, dear boy. I understand the ambient temperature in some of those mountain passes when the wind blows can dip below minus fifty Fahrenheit.''

''I had heard minus seventy, but no matter. We do what we must.''

''You should pen a monograph on neo-stoicism someday when you have the time,'' said Chesterton with a laugh. Zulu simply turned and walked out. Chesterton had been wrong—it did hurt when he laughed.

4

Stone Hudson peered up at the gray sky. There would be more snow, and while it would be to his advantage in getting in, it would hinder him in getting out. But once the troublesome Dan Track and his woman Desiree Goth were taken care of, he would have several days to rendezvous with the Master.

It was a stroke of luck. He climbed out of the cab of the Chevy pickup and started walking across the runway, pulling up the cowl hood of his parka, arranging it around his face against the wind. A stroke of luck, but he distrusted luck. A couple of things had come too easily: the Consortium had sent Track's nephew to investigate the deaths near the factory at Idatana City, and an old friend had been talking to a drunken bush pilot and learned that a tall, well-muscled man with a mustache and a dark-haired woman who sounded European and was a raving beauty had been dropped off in Twisted Oak, Idaho. It paid to be thorough, Hudson told himself, walking toward the converted DC-7, the aircraft that would deposit him with his thirteen men within a few miles of the mountain A frame Track and his woman had rented under falsified names.

Luck. He considered that. It was luck, to a certain degree at least, that he worked for the Master, and that the Directorate would need him.

Good luck.

And it was bad luck for everybody else.

He shivered, not from the cold but from the thought.

It was an ingenious weapon, certainly. A nerve gas that contained a bacterial agent. The gas would kill and then as the gas broke down chemically, the bacterial agent would evolve and kill again. And then the bacterial agent would break down into something totally harmless.

It was like the effect of a neutron bomb as the Master had explained it to him. Kill all that lived and preserve the real estate. And never leave a trace for analysis. Hudson liked the efficiency of the thing. He wondered, as he walked, how many cities would it take for the Master to ensure supremacy. First there would be Seattle. Then Atlanta and Indianapolis. And then the Master would issue his ultimatum, that any city at his will could be murdered. It would likely be some time before the United States government would surrender. Other cities would have to die. But there were hundreds of spots that could be given the treatment without crippling the nation's economy.

Millions of deaths. Perhaps that many. But then the Master would have what he wanted, the most powerful nation on Earth as his seat of power.

Hudson stopped shortly before reaching the fuselage. His father had been a minister. He suddenly remembered one of his father's sermons given on a hot summer morning when the young Hudson would rather have been fishing or humping the girl across town who'd let you jump her for a pack of cigarettes.

The sermon had dealt with the Antichrist.

And now Hudson thought of the Master of D.E.A.T.H.

He shook his head. His father's crazy religious beliefs wouldn't get to him. He kept walking, then climbed aboard the aircraft. There was work to do.

5

He was cold. It was too early in the day for Jack Daniel's and Coke and so he slowed in front of the restaurant, the four-wheel-drive Jeep Cherokee skidding a little. He didn't drink coffee usually. Sometimes hot tea. But a bowl of soup, a hamburger and a glass of milk would do pretty nicely just about now. He studied the sign. Bar-B-Q. They'd probably have hamburgers. He wouldn't trust his stomach to unknown barbecue sauce. He glanced into the rearview. One other vehicle was moving—a Jeep like his at the far end of the town's main street, but this Jeep with Mars lights on the top. The cops.

He edged the Jeep forward, not wanting to be stuck on the ice. He had gotten stuck in a snowdrift coming into the town and had nearly frozen to death getting out. There were some conditions even a four-wheel drive could not cope with. And no telephone service in the last town thirty miles back. No motel, either.

He angled the Jeep into a parking slot beside a drift-covered vehicle that might have been a pickup truck and evidently hadn't been moved since the last snowfall two days earlier. He shut off the engine and zipped his parka against the wind that would be howling. He pulled up the hood and stepped from the Jeep, watching his footing; it was slippery. To the left of the Jeep, on the driver's side and close enough to him that he could only open his door two-thirds of the way, was a state police car.

He slammed the door on the Jeep and locked it, pocketing the keys in his coat.

He slogged ahead, purchasing himself against the left front fender of the Jeep as he scrambled up from the lot and over a plough drift, half sliding down onto the ice-slick sidewalk, balancing himself and standing stock-still. He started to edge across the icy sidewalk, reaching toward the steamed-over window of the restaurant, balancing himself against the glass. All that showed through the steam was an orange neon sign reading Miller's. The last thing he wanted was a cold beer.

He crept along over the ice, the cold numbing to him now. There was a rack outside and he could see two pairs of skis and two sets of poles. "Idiots." George Beegh laughed. He skied and he knew what the slip-stream could feel like on the skin even in good weather.

The thought chilled him. He crept ahead, reaching the glass double doors of the café, shoving the right one open inward, then stepping inside. There was a rubber mat and he wiped his feet on it as he closed the door behind him against the wind. The floor looked slippery from brown streaks of slush and he walked across it carefully. Three men sat at the counter. There were booths along the far wall and he couldn't tell if any of them were occupied.

He had been alone in the Jeep for hours. He headed for the counter. He straddled a swiveling red-vinyl-covered stool and pulled his feet up onto the step. One of the three men was wearing a hunter's cap cocked back over a lined forehead, the man's age indeterminate but advanced, a huge hand at the end of a bony wrist protruding from a leather jacket and holding a mug of what looked like coffee. The man noticed him staring. "Howdy."

George smiled. "Hi. Crappy weather out there."

"Yep," and the man looked back to his coffee.

He looked to his left. The two other men he could see now were state policemen, heavy coats only partially obscuring their service revolvers. One of them turned to him. "You just come in from over by the Montana border?"

"Yeah—not just though. Took me a while."

"I'm surprised you made it at all. Roads north and west of here are already impassable."

"The ones south and east of here aren't too much better." George laughed. He climbed down from the stool and extended his right hand. "Name's George Beegh."

"George B...what? Didn't catch it."

"No, my last name's Beegh. B-E-E-G-H."

"Oh...sorry." The trooper climbed down from his stool and took George's hand. "I'm Harry Burkowitz and this is Ralph Fletcher. State Patrol. We maybe just became the local police until this snow clears up. Our car's about done for with this weather."

"Hi." The second state patrol officer grinned, not getting up, but sticking out his right hand. "George, is it?"

"Right."

"Pull up a stool, George." The first policeman smiled. George sat down beside him.

A waitress came up and handed him a mug of coffee and shot him a smile. He mentally shrugged. Maybe a little coffee would warm him up. "Thanks. You make hamburgers?"

"Best in town," she said, smiling. She was in her late thirties or early forties and had a kind of warm glow to her face under the short cropped brown hair.

"Only ones in town," the trooper named Harry said with a laugh.

"Still the best," she replied. "Want some cheese on it?"

"Yeah, please, and some french fries, and what kind of soup you got?"

"Anything Campbell's makes less we're out of it."

"How about vegetable beef or something like that. I lose track of the names."

"Somethin' like that. Right, you got it."

"And a glass of milk, too, huh?" He'd sipped at the coffee and thought better of it.

"Right," and she walked off.

"What brings you out in this weather, George?" Harry asked.

George reached into his right breast pocket under his parka, passing over the ID case.

"You an insurance dick?" Ralph asked, peering over Harry's shoulder.

"Yeah, like that."

"Whatchya doin' out here?"

But the one named Ralph cut in, talking across the lip of his coffee mug. "That fella that went off the road and crashed his pickup truck and when they found him he had this green-colored fungus stuff all over him—right?"

"You got it." George nodded. He didn't plan to tell the police any more than he had to.

"There were a couple other deaths like that between some town named Twisted Oak and through here and down into Idatana over on the border." There had been fifteen, and in each case the fungus had as yet been impervious to analysis by the Centers for Disease Control or any of the private scientific laboratories and medical research facilities the Consortium had enlisted. Of the fifteen, eleven had been insured by Consortium member companies.

"The Consortium's a group of the world's largest insurance underwriters. They're the people I work for. Some of the people who died and had that fungus stuff on them were insured by some of the member companies. They asked me to check it out."

"Well, young fella," the one named Harry said, lowering his voice conspiratorially, "it could be we got us some Russians up to some no good shit, ya know?"

George raised his eyebrows, then shrugged his shoulders. "Hope not," he said sincerely.

"That guy looked like he died with a lot of hurt," Ralph volunteered.

The hamburger came, George lifting up the top of the bun. The pickle set in the middle of the melted slice of American cheese was the color of the green stuff that had been all over the body he had seen behind glass in Atlanta at the Centers for Disease Control before following up on the assignment from Chesterton. He poured ketchup over it so he wouldn't see it.

"Maybe it's people from outer space," Harry suggested with a smile.

"Naw, I saw that movie," George volunteered. "The guys didn't look anything like this."

"Well," Harry began, swallowing coffee, George watching his Adam's apple bob up and down, "it's whoever or whatever killed old Bliss Saunders in his pickup truck. You packin'?"

"It depends on whether or not you're gonna check if I've got the right paperwork to do it in Idaho." George grinned, taking a bite of the cheeseburger. He wondered where the soup was, and as he looked up it arrived.

"No, your credentials look good enough."

"A 9mm and a .45 and a few other things in the Jeep outside." There wasn't any sense lying. A smart cop could usually spot a gun no matter how well you hid it, and George hadn't deluded himself that one or both of the Idaho state troopers hadn't spotted one or both of his.

"Hell." Ralph laughed. "After I saw old Bliss Saunders, well, I tossed my Super Blackhawk in the trunk of the car."

George tried the soup—it was hot and wasn't watered down and she had given him the whole can. He looked at the breakfront holster that Harry wore. The revolver looked like a K-Frame Smith & Wesson. "Model 65?"

Harry grinned. "You got a good eye, Mr. Beegh."

"George—call me George."

"George—yeah, 65s with 110-grain .38 Special plus P pluses in 'em. Good load, but right beside old Ralph's .44 Ruger, well, I got my 6-inch 629 loaded with 240-grainers I make up myself—cast lead. Use 'em huntin' sometimes. Figured it wouldn't hurt to bring along the gun and a coupla boxes of my ammo just in case."

"Well...my uncle, he's kinda in the same business I am," George told them. "He uses a SPAS-12 a lot of the time. I've got one in the car, loaded up with Federal Super Slugs—maybe for the same reason you guys got your .44s." George took another spoonful of soup. Mmm good, he thought, smiling.

"SPAS-12," Ralph said. "That is that big police shotgun Arnold Schwarzenegger was using in that movie, right?"

"Yeah." George nodded. "Good movie. Good gun." He took a bite of the cheeseburger, feeling like the last of the two-fisted eaters, the cheeseburger in his left hand, the soup spoon in his right. "Who those skis belong to outside?"

"Couple over there," and Ralph gestured with his left thumb over his shoulder toward the booths against the far wall.

George glanced over his left shoulder. The man wore a beard, and the woman's hair was auburn instead of blond. But it was Sergei Baslovitch and his bride Tatiana. George started to choke on his soup.

"HE SAW US. It *is* him," Tatiana whispered.

Baslovitch nodded, making a show of looking toward the counter and calling out with the best German accent he could muster, "Sandy—could I have more coffee, please?" And he stood up. He had to gamble George was using his right name. "George! George! How are you? It's me—Peter!" And he started across the room, extending his right hand. "Peter Kroehler, George! And Louise is with me." He was beside the counter and pumping George's right hand, George having dropped the soup spoon into his bowl.

"You know George here?" Harry enthused.

"Ahh—of course I do, Harry," and Baslovitch grinned at George...hoping.

George's face lit with a smile, his dark eyes bright. "Yeah, you know us insurance dicks, we get around a lot."

George had left him the opening to establish the relationship background and Baslovitch jumped into it before either Harry or his partner could say anything. "Yeah—George here—we worked together on a case when I was with the West German police. So, George—you are still with your previous employer?"

He was giving George an opening back.

"Yeah. Hey, I bet you remember my Uncle Dan. Well, we still work for Sir Abner. Dan and Desiree are on vacation, in this neck of the woods, too. How about you and—"

"Louise," Baslovitch supplied in case George had forgotten. "We live here, higher in the mountains. We skied down. The roads were impassable."

"Tell me about it," George said with a laugh.

Baslovitch heard the footsteps behind him. He didn't look around. It would be Tatiana picking things up. "George, you still look so handsome," and she passed him and put her arms around George. Baslovitch smiled. George was still holding his hamburger.

"Louise." George smiled. "Wow, you look just great."

Ralph spoke, "Talk about a small world, huh."

"It is that, yes," Baslovitch genuinely agreed. He wondered if it was too small.

"Listen," Harry began, "we're gonna try gettin' the car goin' again if we can. If we can't, gonna go over to the police station and check in with Marty Goodwin—he's the chief here—and use his radio to call in. I got a feelin' we'll be seein' you," and Harry stood up, extending his right hand. Baslovitch watched as George shook with Harry and then with Ralph.

"Peter—good seein' you and Louise again."

Baslovitch smiled, clapping Harry on the shoulder. "Listen, once the weather clears and the roads are usable, why don't you and Ralph come up to our place for lunch. And I'm not trying to ruin your business," he called over George's shoulder to Sandy behind the counter.

"Likely story." She laughed.

"Hey, we'd like that, Peter," Ralph said with a smile. "Louise," and he nodded to Baslovitch's wife.

The two state troopers started for the door, Baslovitch's wife saying, "Don't forget lunch!"

"Got a deal, Louise," Ralph called back, grinning.

Baslovitch looked at George. He could hear the door to the street closing. "George, come sit with us. We can talk over old times."

"Sure," and George set down his hamburger. Baslovitch picked up the glass of milk, Tatiana took the bowl of soup and George took the plate with the hamburger and the uneaten french fries.

"Do you want the ketchup, George?" Tatiana asked.

"Yeah, here, I'll—"

"No, I have it." She smiled, starting back to the booth.

Baslovitch walked beside George, George hissing under his breath, "This is where you guys live?"

"Yes. We were watching you before you noticed us. Tatiana spotted you. Call her Louise, or Louie," and he laughed. "And I am Peter. Kroehler. K-R-O-E-H-L-E-R. Retired from the West German National Police. Independently wealthy. She's my recent bride."

"Gotchya," George said, nodding.

Baslovitch sat where he had been sitting, Tatiana opposite him, George squeezing in beside her. Tatiana smiled, whispering, "It's good to see you again, George. It really is. We miss our old friends."

"Look, I'll get outa here as soon as I can. I don't wanna screw you guys up," George whispered.

"Yes, terrible weather," Baslovitch said, raising his voice.

It was Sandy. "You forgot your coffee, mister."

"Oh, thanks," George said with a smile.

Sandy left the table and George whispered, "I don't usually drink coffee, but I mean this is really yech—"

Baslovitch laughed. "But the food is good. Next time order tea. She can't hurt that. What are you doing here? The weather is terrible. I'm surprised you made it in from wherever you came."

He watched as George licked his lips, seemed to study his soup bowl, then looked up. "Well—"

"Let him eat first," Tatiana supplied. "I don't think any of us are going anywhere. Look!"

Baslovitch looked over his shoulder. As the one door to the café opened, Sandy's daughter coming in swathed

in scarves and a near ankle-length coat, he could see the
snow swirling outside.

The blizzard had come again.

He waved at Sandy's teenage daughter and then
turned to watch George eat.

6

Dan Track stared out the picture window that fronted the A frame's great room. "It's snowing again, really coming down."

From behind him, he could hear Desiree say, "This is more snow than I've ever seen in Switzerland."

"This is more snow than I've ever seen, period," Track said, shaking his head. "Very romantic." He smiled, turning around, staring across the great room toward the off-white sectional that made an L in the middle of the room and was separated from the massive flagstone hearth by a dark brown fur rug. Desiree was crocheting an afghan, if he remembered properly. Another afghan covered her legs stretched out across the sofa. "Just think—the two of us, marooned here by a blizzard. Plenty of firewood—"

"A good thing you cut some this morning."

"Chain saws scare me to death." He smiled, stabbing his hands into the pockets of his Levi's and starting away from the window and across the room toward her. "But plenty of wood for the fire."

"The propane tanks are comforting, too, though," she said.

"I'll start again. Plenty of wood for the fire, plenty of food, plenty of stuff to drink, and just you and me," he told her, bending over her on the sectional, tilting her chin up so he could kiss her.

"Is this what life will be like when we're married?"

"What? Snowbound?"

"No. I mean…just you and I."

"Well, maybe a few ahh…you know…the patter of little feet?"

"Mice wearing overshoes?"

Track laughed. "Do you like life like this?" he asked her suddenly.

"Mmm-hmm," she murmured as Track sat down beside her. She put down her crocheting and twisted around on the sofa to face him. He held her hands in his. "I like life like this very much. And how about you?"

He smiled, touching his lips to her forehead, smoothing back her almost black hair, looking into the blueness of her eyes. "You know I do."

"I'm glad for all this snow. We would have left tomorrow."

"I've got to get him before he gets us," Track told her.

"Zulu will find some lead on Hudson, and that will lead us to the Master."

"Lead me," Track told her. "He plays too rough."

"You're thinking about George and Ellen, about Ellen being paralyzed."

"Yeah," Track almost whispered.

"I talked with Ellen before we came up here. I called her in the hospital. She sounded genuinely happy."

"Marrying George? She must have taken one in the head, too."

"That's a terrible thing to say. George is your nephew."

"That's why I say terrible things about him." Track smiled, and then he let the smile go. "Yeah, I think about Ellen. I don't want anything happening to you."

"Nothing will happen to me. I have you, remember?"

Track lowered his head toward her, resting his forehead in her hair, closing his eyes. Her hair smelled like perfume—something terribly expensive and terribly good to smell. "And I have you and I'm keeping you," Track told her.

"Do you know that you haven't picked up a gun all day long?"

"What?"

"The .45 beside the bed, it's still beside the bed."

"You mean I'm getting careless," he told her.

"No, I don't mean that. Hold me." She leaned up toward him and he folded his arms around her very tightly. A log split in the fireplace with a loud crack and he could hear the crackle of sparks. He still held her.

STONE HUDSON SAT ON A CRATE in the center of the aisle formed between the benches that flanked the interior of the fuselage. "All right, we're gonna go over it one more time." He studied the faces of the thirteen men. "We bail out at twenty-five thousand and we pop the chutes at seven hundred fifty feet. We've got to be precise or one of us is going to wind up wearin' one of the snowmobiles on his head, right guys?"

There were nods and grunts.

"Okay. Each man is responsible for his own weapons during the jump. Once we're down, Hatfield and Sears—what do you do?"

Hatfield, red haired, looking like a kid out of high school last Thursday, grinned. "Me and Bobby Sears secure our chutes, and while the rest of you guys go after the snowmobiles, we go after the special-weapons chest. We open it up, check that the LAW rockets and the other shit didn't get damaged none, then by that time, the rest of you guys are on the scene. We hand out

the stuff and we get on our snowmobile and ride off into
the sunset.''

"Right, but it'll be considerably after sunset. We
use the snowmobiles until we reach what point,
McCormick?''

McCormick grinned, his teeth ridiculously white-
looking against his black face. Hudson didn't like
blacks, but they fought well. McCormick nodded once,
then began. "We ditch the snowmobiles five miles from
the target at the coordinates on our maps. One man
stays with each of the snowmobiles and the other seven
set off on cross-country skis to the target.''

"Right," and he looked at Greenwald who would be
his second in command on the forward element. "What
do we do, Greenwald?''

"All right, Colonel. You lead us to the target. Once
we get to the rise overlooking the rear face of the target, we split into two fire teams and flank the house. On
your signal, we give 'em everything we've got. If they
make it outa the house alive, they're right into our killing ground. We make it that way when you fire for effect a couple of the LAW rockets so they think we've got
'em on three sides. We flush 'em into the kill zone and
blow 'em away.''

"You forgot the most important part, Greenwald,''
Stone Hudson hissed. "We check the bodies. Even if we
gotta wait for the house to stop burnin' to do it. We've
got to be sure. I've got dental records on Major Track
and the Goth dame. We've got to be sure.''

"Why some ex-Army guy and a broad so important,
Colonel?''

It was McCormick.

"Because, man," Hudson said, "if anybody slips up
and this Major Track or the woman doesn't kill him, I
will. Now grab smokes if you want. The lamp's lit till

we're ten minutes from the drop zone.'' Hudson began looking to his personal gear.

He picked up his Beretta 92SB, dropped the magazine and checked the spring tension by pushing down on the top round. He cycled the action several times. He had lubricated the pistol especially well against the cold, as had all his men done with their weapons.

He pushed the magazine up the well and made sure it was locked, then holstered it in the Cattle Baron Leather shoulder rig under his left armpit. He checked an identical Beretta in the same way. This one he replaced in the flap holster that would go on his right hip.

He checked the assault rifle—the M-16 was as good as an M-16 could be. He had personally tested all of the assault rifles issued for the exercise.

He set it down.

This time it had to be done right. He had come to respect the talents of this Major Track—talents aimed at foiling the plans of the Master and the Directorate. D.E.A.T.H. could no longer tolerate the man to live. And neither could he. It was a personal thing now. He was the best at what he did, and once Major Daniel Hunter Track was dead there would be no one to dispute it, no one at all.

7

They had made the refueling stop in Denver and Chesterton had used the time to stretch his legs. When he kept moving, the rib slash actually bothered him less and the new bandaging had made a marked improvement in his comfort. He sat in the passenger seat opposite Zulu. He watched as the giant Oxford-educated black methodically cleaned his Browning Hi-Power. "We could have contacted the police via radio, of course," Chesterton said half to himself.

"Excellent. We tell them that even though they are snowbound and cannot get out to do their normal rounds, cannot get out to meet emergency situations, they should somehow reach into the mountains miles from the nearest town and be prepared to repel an assault by trained commandos. The size of the assault group undetermined, their arrival time unspecified."

"I know. I know all that," Chesterton said dismissively. "But I'd like to be doing something rather than just riding in this very comfortable little airplane."

"Soon we will, Sir Abner. My concern is as great as yours—perhaps greater."

"Desiree—yes, I know."

"Desiree is my family. You lost a sweetheart, you told me once. I lost a wife, children. I lost all my family, my tribe. I am the only one left. And Desiree means more to me than my life. I have come to accept Major Track."

Chesterton said it before thinking. "Do you love her?"

He looked at Zulu, and then he looked away.

Zulu's voice sounded strained somehow as he answered. "I count you as my friend, Sir Abner. A comrade in arms of the highest order. Someone whom I would die for, as well. Never ask me that again, sir."

"I'm sorry, really I am."

"I am aware of that. But I'll answer your question, because a question once asked and never answered lingers in the mind, perhaps becoming an obsession. I came to love her, but I know that I cannot. Tell no one." And he looked at Chesterton from across the aisle.

Chesterton looked into Zulu's black eyes. "When you were made, Zulu, God broke the mold."

8

George had gotten his thermal-insulated hooded sweat shirt from the Jeep, then walked—half skated—with Baslovitch and Tatiana across the main street to the General Merchandise Store. After telling Sergei and Tatiana—he reminded himself to try to think of them as Peter and Louise—the reason for his coming, about the mysterious deaths, his assignment from the Consortium, he had listened to the radio the woman in the café had turned on. An additional fourteen to eighteen inches of snow were predicted overnight, the temperature dropping to something he had mentally rejected.

Baslovitch clambered over the snowbank and then helped Tatiana over. "Do you need any help, George?"

"Naw, I'm fine," and George started up, his balance beginning to go, but Baslovitch's hands were out and George crashed into him, just missing slipping to the sidewalk.

"Our friends Andy Mistral and his son Morgan have a Sno-Cat. Maybe they can get us up to our house and you can stay with us."

"And if they can't—" Tatiana laughed "—then we'll all need a place to stay."

"No motel here, either, right?"

"This isn't exactly a place for tourists. There's a motel fifty miles from here—a nice enough one, too, really—but you'd never make it, even with four-wheel drive." Baslovitch turned the knob on the general store's front door and held it open, letting Tatiana pass through, George following her.

"Hello? Andy?"

George looked around as Tatiana called; the store appeared deserted. It was an odd-looking place, he thought. Winchester and Marlin lever-action rifles and a few miscellaneous bolt actions were racked on the wall behind the counter, neatly stacked red-and-white boxes of Federal ammunition were arranged beneath and surrounding the rack. A second rack held shot-guns—pumps and semiautos mostly—and beneath and around this was stacked more ammo. Beside him as he moved toward the center of the single aisle was a wooden "horse" made of rough-hewn log pieces, and on the horse was a saddle. Assorted other items of tack were to his left. Bags of grain were to his right. He reached out and touched the saddle—the feel of the leather was good. Groceries were everywhere: canned goods, boxes of cereal. To the right on the far wall was a bank of white porcelain freezer-refrigerator units, vertical models except for one horizontal model—he imagined that was for meat. To the left in the back were yard goods and some clothing. It looked like a basic mixture of men's wear and women's wear.

General Merchandise. He smiled, wondering how many stores such as this remained in America. Not many, he ventured.

"Andy? Morgan?"

Baslovitch's voice had taken up the chant.

"Maybe something's wrong. I mean, do people lock up around here if they leave their stores?"

"Usually, but just to let people know they are not in," Tatiana answered without looking at him. "Andy? Morgan?"

The door opened from the street behind them, George wheeling toward the sound. "Hey, Peter."

It was Ralph, the state trooper.

"Ralph?"

"You're lookin' for Andy, right?"

"Or Morgan," Tatiana chimed in. "We wanted to thumb a ride in the Sno-Cat up to our house."

"Yeah, well..." Ralph began. "Well—"

"What is it?" Baslovitch asked.

"Morgan was out in the truck, delivering some groceries to Mrs. Cahill up on the other side of town...Eben Cahill's widow. Ya know her?"

"We met her once at church," Tatiana said.

"Church?" George asked incredulously.

Tatiana patted his forearm with her hand and smiled.

"Morgan was on his way back," Ralph began again. "Called his dad on the CB radio, told him he was feeling kinda sick, some kinda cloud around him. And then the radio died. Andy hotfooted it outa here in the Cat. The chief just got a call on his CB. Andy's out there screamin' and cussin' and cryin'. Morgan's dead. Covered up with some kinda green funguslike stuff."

"Oh my God," Tatiana whispered.

"I want to see it," George told the trooper.

"Figured you would, George. And Peter—we got no backup, no medical examiners—nothin'. Figured you bein' a retired cop and all...well..."

"Of course," Baslovitch murmured. "Morgan was a fine boy. This is terrible."

"I'll come, too," Tatiana volunteered.

"Can't, Louise—only got two snowmobiles available. Harry's warming 'em up now. Me and Harry can take one, Peter and George here can take the other. You can stay with the chief. He's the only one down at the police station and he could use some help if you don't mind."

"Yes, yes of course. I'll do whatever I can."

"Kinda figured you would."

And then Baslovitch did something George hadn't expected. He turned to Tatiana and said, "Darling, you don't have a gun, do you?"

"No...."

Baslovitch looked to Ralph. "We'll take her down to the station. I want her armed. Whatever this is, she may need to be."

"You got a gun on, Peter?"

"I always do." Baslovitch nodded resolutely. "I always do."

9

Perhaps it was Desiree's remark about not having touched a gun all day, but while she worked on dinner, he watched a portion of his friend Trapper's new videotape series on advanced pistolsmithing. Dan Track squatted on the off-white woven rug about eight feet back from the television set, sipping at a double shot of Seagrams with a splash, watching Trapper's hands begin the action tuning process on a Colt Python. During his lifetime of fooling with guns in one way or another—using them for recreational shooting or just to stay alive—he had never done anything more complicated in the gunsmithing area than replace a broken extractor in a .45, or a new firing pin and firing pin spring, or pop the sideplate off a Smith revolver to get at the internal workings when the gun had needed truly dramatic cleaning. The tape fascinated him.

"Dan—could you give me a hand?"

"Just a sec," he called back. Getting to his feet, he went to the VCR, pushed a bewildering array of buttons and watched for the power light to fade. As he started across the room, he glanced to his right through the picture window. The snow was still falling, the flakes the size of half dollars now, drifting like a curtain of lace across the window in swirls made by the wind. "We're getting one hell of a snowfall out there."

"It's pretty."

"Hate to be stuck out in it. Before I turned on the tape I caught a station from somewhere—the temperature's supposed to drop like a stone in a well tonight."

He stopped by the side of the kitchen counter, and looked past her to the back door. "I wouldn't want to try opening that door in a hurry. The wind's blowing from the north, and the snow has probably drifted up to the second floor by now."

"Give me a hand with this, will you?"

He walked around the counter, setting down his drink. He looked at her. She wore an ankle-length wool plaid skirt, the colors varying shades of gray. The sweater she wore, round necked with three-quarter-length sleeves, was gray as well. Over the sweater and the skirt she wore a long, bib-fronted apron with a design embroidered in a band approximately at the level of her breasts and the same design repeated an inch or so from the bottom hem. She was pretty.

"I thought you told me I was terrible in the kitchen. What do you want me to help with?" Track asked.

"I have given up on wearing out my arm muscles. I put the turkey in the upper oven to settle, and I almost killed myself getting it in there."

"Okay," he said as he smiled.

"Here, you'll need these," and she handed him two pot holders.

As she opened the upper oven door, he asked her, "Where do you want it?"

"Over there on the counter, near where you put your drink."

Track nodded. He had never understood how women did it, you still burned your hands even with the pot holders. But he got the turkey down and shifted it onto the counter. "Need any more help?"

"Just in eating it," she said.

"I'll volunteer for that," he told her enthusiastically. "And I'll even get the wine." He had begun chilling the champagne that morning when she had started preparing the turkey. They had planned to use whatever was left of the turkey for sandwiches the next day when the bush pilot would have come for them. But he wouldn't be coming—not for several days, Track realized. There would be no place to land in Twisted Oak or near it, and even if there was, the four-wheel-drive International Travelall that Track had rented along with the house wouldn't be able to get them down the mountain. He was happy; he liked turkey leftovers.

DINNER WAS A MEMORY, a warm feeling in his stomach. Desiree had sat beside him on the couch looking at the fireplace most of the night. He had read for a while, an adventure novel by Josh Culhane, one of the books in The Takers series. When Desiree stirred beside him, Track had told her, "That guy Sean Dodge in The Takers—he leads a charmed life," and he had laughed, setting the book down on the floor.

Desiree snuggled closer then, and they had watched the fire for nearly another hour. "I'll be sorry to leave here," she whispered, Track feeling her breath in his left ear.

"So will I. Why don't we come back, spend a few more weeks here after we nail—"

She touched her fingers to his lips. "Shh."

He kissed her fingertips. "All right, I won't say it."

"Come to bed?"

He turned around toward her and looked into her eyes. "But the couch is already so nice and warm," and he drew her face toward his, touching her mouth, then pulling her closer to him, kissing her.

He felt her hands at the bottom of his sweater, pushing it up, popping the snaps of his shirt, her fingers against the flesh of his abdomen. His right hand began to move along the length of her left leg, to the hem of her skirt, then beneath it. His hand started moving up her bare leg, bunching up the slip, the skirt, the apron she still wore, his hand stopping, sliding across the silk of her panties and stopping at the waistband. But his hand only stopped for an instant, and then he pulled them down. Her hands were something alive that he could feel, entwining in his hair, brushing at his face as his lips touched her neck. The heat of her was unreal.

SERGEI BASLOVITCH'S SKIN felt numb with the cold as he stepped off the snowmobile, the Sno-Cat less than three yards away. Ralph, the state patrolman, was already off. In the swirling snow, the snow made that much more vivid in the cones of the headlights of the snowmobiles, Baslovitch could faintly make out the shape of the pickup truck a few yards beyond the Cat.

"I don't see Andy!" Ralph shouted over the noise of the second snowmobile. Baslovitch looked over his shoulder; George and Harry, the other state trooper, were coming up. "Maybe Andy's in the truck with his boy."

"Yes, perhaps," Baslovitch agreed. "You and Harry check the Sno-Cat; George and I will check the truck." And Baslovitch called to George who was climbing off his snowmobile.

George started toward him with a massive black flashlight in his hand. Baslovitch flicked on his own borrowed flashlight, lifting his left foot out of the drift, then plunging it down, then the right foot, then the left. He wore a borrowed parka over his own ski clothes, more as an accommodation to Ralph and Harry, because the ski clothes had been warm enough. The parka was open, blowing in the howling wind of the blizzard, and Baslovitch tugged off his right ski mitten with his

teeth, tucking it in the pocket of the parka. The thin silk
glove he had worn beneath the mitten would be warm
enough for a few moments, he told himself. He reached
under his own ski parka, finding the butt of the P-5, his
fist closing around the Walther. He kept moving. He
glanced to his left, and saw George trudging through the
drifted snow beside him, George with the Colt Combat
Government in his right fist, no glove on at all.

"What do you think?" George shouted to him.

"I don't know, George. We'll see."

"I mean, you think it could be Russians?"

Baslovitch stopped moving and looked at George.
"That is always a possibility." He kept his voice low
enough so that only George could hear.

"When I was in KGB there were many secret proj-
ects I would not have needed to know about. This could
be one of them. But if the Soviets were doing this and
their responsibility in the matter was discovered, it
would be an act of war. So, I don't think so." He shut
up then and walked on, fighting the drifts. On his right,
Baslovitch saw that the two state troopers had already
reached the Sno-Cat. The light in one of their hands—
because of the swirl of snow Baslovitch could make out
no faces—zigzagged through the air, left to right.
Nothing in the Cat. Ralph and Harry were coming at a
tangent to meet them at the pickup truck.

Baslovitch and George had narrowed the distance to
the pickup truck to five yards, but the height of the
snowdrifts around them on what had once been a road
made each moment torture. "I should have brought my
skis—it would have been faster," Baslovitch called to
George. But he didn't know if George had heard him.

Four yards.

Three.

Two yards, and then another long step, up and out of
one drift and into another. Baslovitch sagged against

the left front fender of the truck. He called to George. He was sweating, mildly out of breath from the exertion. "Don't touch anything with your bare hand, George, and don't touch Andy Mistral with your bare hand, either. We don't know what this substance is or how long it remains virulent."

"All right, but you be careful."

Baslovitch nodded, too exhausted to keep talking.

He could not see inside the cab of the pickup truck because of the snow that had drifted across the hood and over the windshield. He tried the passenger side— it opened.

And a body fell into the snow. "Don't touch him, George!"

The face was gray and frozen. Blood had frozen or coagulated beside the right temple. Locked into the right hand was Morgan Mistral's pistol. But the hand it was locked into was that of Andy Mistral, Morgan's father.

"He—he—"

"Killed himself," Baslovitch supplied. "Morgan's mother died when Morgan was a baby. Andy didn't have anybody except Morgan—had nobody." Baslovitch closed his eyes, shaking his head. And then he opened his eyes, stepping over the body of Andy Mistral. Mechanically, he had observed that there was no green funguslike substance visible on the elder Mistral's skin. Baslovitch shone the light inside the pickup's cab. The face was blood smeared, and there was an impact circle on the windshield, blood and spiderwebbed glass. Baslovitch stared at the skin that was not blood flecked. It was splotched with green, the green the consistency of mold.

Baslovitch heard Ralph's voice outside the cab, "Holy shit."

Baslovitch whispered to the dead boy, "I am sorry, Morgan," and then raised his voice. "Look in here but don't touch him—don't touch anything."

And he moved aside. Harry shouldered past him. "My God."

"Yeah," Baslovitch muttered. "Harry, tell me if the window on the driver's side is partially down."

"About an inch, Peter."

"Without touching Morgan's body—or anything else—can you see if the left side of his face has more of the green splotches than the right?"

"No, I can't. Yeah...wait. It does."

Baslovitch nodded, then turned to George, then looked at Harry and Ralph. "I would say we are dealing with a gas, but something the like of which I have never seen, never heard of. Purportedly the boy told his father on the CB radio of some sort of cloud. Evidently the gas made the boy lose control of the vehicle. From the minimal amount of blood on the face where Morgan's head hit the windshield, I would say Morgan was dead before his head struck the glass."

George's voice interrupted him. "According to what we know about this green stuff, it's some form of bacteria—lethal. But we don't know what. They were able to reactivate some of it with some kind of radiation treatment in one of the labs the Consortium has working on this thing. The fungus spread and killed seven rats in ten seconds. But once the supply of radiation was cut off, the fungus didn't spread anymore."

"Something that has a very short life," Baslovitch thought aloud. "Probably a gas that affects the central nervous system."

"Most of the victims died of suffocation."

"That would fit," Baslovitch said. "And then the gas turns into some sort of bacteria that is very short-lived.

That's why you don't have an epidemic resulting from these deaths. Hmm. Yet."

"The Russians, Peter?" Harry asked.

"If the Russians had something this advanced," Baslovitch said confidently, "they would have tested it in Afghanistan or elsewhere, not here...I don't think."

"Maybe it is something from, uh, up there," Ralph said slowly, pointing skyward.

"Little green men with a little green fungus? I don't think so. If it were accidental contagion, it would be more widespread. And I don't believe in little green men."

"He only believes in little blue men," George said. When no one laughed, George added, "Just trying to brighten things up a little."

Baslovitch closed his eyes a moment to think. He opened them, the cold numbing him still. "Was there anything else Morgan told his father—anything Andy repeated? Anything at all?"

"No...yeah. Before that cloud thing, he heard some kinda noise in the sky and looked up to see."

"Some kind of noise in the sky," Baslovitch repeated. "Some kind of noise in the sky."

10

"I was freezing my tuschie off up there, let me tell you." Jilly Mason laughed, sipping at his gin. "But it really worked, just like you said it would," and he smiled at the man who had engineered his escape from jail, the man who called himself the Master of D.E.A.T.H.

"Didn't I tell you, mein Herr—he is the very best helicopter pilot anywhere!" Klaus Gurnheim clapped the Master on the shoulder and started to stand up.

The Master's eyes took on an icy look and he turned his face to look up at Klaus Gurnheim. "Herr Gurnheim, I appreciate your enthusiasm vastly, however, if you ever touch me again without my specific permission, I shall have you killed in some manner most unpleasant."

"Yes—yes, mein Herr."

"Now, sit down."

Mason was amused.

"Tell me, Mr. Mason—what was the timing again?"

"Well, I activated the spray and despite the snow in just ten seconds the pickup truck was zigzagging all over the road and into the ditch—fantastic. This stuff you've got... Hey, what can I say?" and Jilly sipped a bit more at his gin.

"I am delighted, truly delighted, Mr. Mason. And you shall be rewarded for your heroism in getting the helicopter airborne in such horrendous weather, aside from the money I am paying you. Herr Gurnheim told me of your preferences.''

''It's pretty obvious, isn't it?'' and Jilly Mason laughed again. The gin was warming him up too fast.

''I took the liberty of procuring—you will pardon the expression—procuring a young boy for you. After you are through with him, he will have to be killed. But you can keep him as long as you like.''

He'd always been transparent, so he knew what his eyes must look like, his lips. ''Where...is the young fella?''

''In the upstairs bedroom at the far end of the hall, Mr. Mason,'' and the Master of D.E.A.T.H. reached across the dining-room table and dangled two keys on a small chain. One was an old-fashioned skeleton key, the other something Jilly Mason recognized all too well—a handcuff key. ''This long key is for the lock on the bedroom door, Mr. Mason. The smaller one unlocks the handcuffs with which we have chained the young man to the bed. Are there any other items you might require?''

Jilly Mason closed his right fist around the key chain. ''No sir, this'll be just fine.''

''Then I take it you are pleased?''

''Yes, I'm very pleased.'' The Master was really good looking, Mason thought. Tall, the eyes piercing, mysterious, the features finely drawn, the arms and the chest well muscled, the rear end tight. ''I'm very pleased.''

The Master let go of the key chain. ''Good. After you have relaxed, we need to discuss something rather important. I'll be occupied for the next several hours. Perhaps we can talk around midnight or so?''

''Yes—yes, I'd like that. Where should I meet you?''

The Master shrugged his broad shoulders. ''I'm afraid the dining room is the most suitable. This is the best house we could find, but no office, no library. Rather Spartan actually.''

"Well..." Jilly began. The Master smiled and Jilly liked what it did to the face. But the eyes always seemed the same. Almost as if they were simultaneously dead and alive. He watched after the Master as he walked from the room.

"He's got a nice ass," Mason hissed to Klaus Gurnheim conspiratorially.

"You are filth. You should be thanking me for having you taken from the federal prison."

"Oh, I do thank you, Klaus. And I thank you for telling him what I like. Prison was really disgusting. I mean—" Mason sipped at his drink, studying the pattern of the wallpaper "—I just never, never had a night's rest." And Mason laughed. "It's hell to be popular!" And he slugged down more of his gin. "What a disgusting place this is. Idatana—what a perfectly horrible name." Mason chuckled as he thought of a joke. "Sounds like somebody threatening to give somebody a spanking. I'd a tan a your hide...." More laughter. "What the hell is this D.E.A.T.H. business, hmm?"

He watched Klaus Gurnheim's face. The old German shrugged his shoulders. "I have learned that D.E.A.T.H. started out many hundreds of years ago. If anybody knows when, nobody has told me so." Gurnheim sighed. "At any event, it was originally called the Directorate. But then about the time of the First World War, someone began calling the organization D.E.A.T.H. The letters stand for the Directorate for Espionage, Assassination, Terrorism and Harassment."

Jilly Mason laughed out loud. "That's absurd! Theatrical—my God!—let me tell you!"

Gurnheim shrugged his shoulders again. "What can I say? He pays well, and if I were to dispute the Master he would have me killed. He was most displeased with me after Major Track neutralized the effectiveness of the bomb I had put aboard the space shuttle—I told you about it.''

Mason stood up; he thought he should while he still could. "All I've got to say is that a rented house in the middle of a blizzard in the middle of nowhere is a funny place for a reunion for a couple of old Nazis like us.'' Mason laughed again. It was the gin doing it, he realized. He started across the room, still holding his glass in one hand, the key ring in the other. ''Idatana!''

11

He hadn't jumped out of an airplane in years and he watched the needle of the altimeter dropping with what he realized was morbid fascination. The winds were too high for any sane person to even consider an airdrop. He smiled to himself—if he and Zulu were sane, he would be very much surprised.

Twelve hundred feet. His fist was already locked to the rip cord of his main chute. He had an auxiliary, but there wouldn't be time to use it. He considered the possibilities: get hung up in some trees, be buried in a snowdrift. He forced himself to think of something else, not daring to take his eyes from the altimeter.

One thousand feet. He gradually drew out the rip cord—at seven hundred fifty, he would pull.

Eight hundred.

Seven hundred fifty. Chesterton tugged the rip cord, his back, his neck, his shoulders, the wound over his rib cage suddenly screaming at him, shouting at him that this was madness. He looked up—the chute had billowed open, and he could feel the winds tearing him southward. They had planned the drop against the wind velocity as well as possible, and now he worked the guides furiously—the ground coming up fast.

In the swirling snow he couldn't see Zulu, but he could faintly make out the dark mass of the half-track snow tractor beneath its four chutes. He braced himself to go into a touchdown in the snow, and he sagged forward into it, but then felt the wrenching pain again— the chute was caught up in the wind.

Chesterton rolled onto his abdomen and chest. If he cut the drag lines, the chute would continue onward, possibly betray their presence in some way or another. He rolled onto his back, trying to dig into the snow and find a purchase. There was none. He looked up, the snow tractor was still falling, and it looked like his line of travel would take him directly under it. No time. The noise be damned, he thought, and he reached for his MPK. It was in a drop case strapped to his chest and he brought the powerful subgun into his right hand. He rammed a magazine up the well and drew back the bolt. He would have one chance, he realized. Looking up, he saw that the tractor was nearly down and he would intersect it and be crushed. He stabbed the MPK into the night and triggered a burst, then another and another, into the center of his billowing parachute, the metal-case 9mms slashing through the fabric, the chute tearing, Chesterton's rate of movement slowing. Another burst and a huge gash appeared in the center of the chute and his movement stopped. The snow tractor shuddered to the ground less than ten yards ahead of him.

Chesterton sagged into the snow.

He looked up and saw Zulu running toward him across the snow, Zulu's black face under the hood of the white snow smock like a formless shadow. Chesterton smiled, calling out to his friend over the wind, "Well, so much for secrecy, eh?" Sir Abner Chesterton started to his feet.

STONE HUDSON RAISED HIS HAND to signal the halt. He dismounted the snowmobile, flapping his arms at his sides to lose some of the stiffness. He looked at McCormick, not envying the man staying with the snow-

mobiles, but not envying himself, either. The thought
of walking five miles in the blizzard, despite the protective clothing, the compasses and the fact they would
be roped together, chilled him more than the cold.

Greenwald approached him.

"What is it?"

"I got the men ready, Colonel. There's some gripin'
about hikin' it out for five miles in this shit!" Greenwald was shouting over the roar of the blizzard.

"We're not takin' any chances," Hudson replied.
"We blow this, we'll be hiking a lot more than five
miles. Track and this Goth woman get away from us, we
gotta hunt them down until they're dead and we're
sure—lead-pipe cinch sure, Greenwald."

"But Colonel, with the wind—"

"With the wind blowing in the same direction we'll
be going, we don't have any idea what kind of sound
might travel. No chances. Any man doesn't want to
come along, fine—he can stay here. Permanently. And
I mean *permanently*."

"Yeah, Colonel, I gotchya."

Hudson nodded, then turned back to the snowmobile. He took up his M-16 and two of the LAW rockets,
his pack never unshouldered along the ten-mile ride
from the drop zone. He leaned into the machine so
McCormick could hear him better. "McCormick—remember, radio silence until this thing is done and we
contact you, unless it's the biggest emergency you could
ever think of, and I better agree with you if you break
silence."

"Right, Colonel. And hey, good luck, man!"

"Yeah." Hudson nodded, slinging the LAW rockets, then starting away from the machine. They would
use flashlights for all except the last mile, and by then
it would be light enough to see unless the blizzard was

so thick that it blotted out any glow at all through the cloud layer. He flicked his Mag-Lite on.

Greenwald came up. "We're set, Colonel!"

"All right, we move out," and Hudson started ahead. He had already checked compass bearings, but in the low visibility—he judged it to be less than an eighth of a mile—it would be a constant thing. But he had allowed two hours additional time for the forced march, considering the conditions.

He started fording through the drifts, the cold already attacking him.

GEORGE BEEGH CLIMBED OUT of the Sno-Cat's cab and back into the wind. The Cat had no heat, but it beat the lashing of the wind one experienced when riding the snowmobiles.

Baslovitch came out on the other side. George reminded himself to think of his old friend as Peter, and he kept repeating this in his mind. The two state troopers followed from George's side of the vehicle.

They had left the snowmobile and the pickup truck, and in the rear of the Sno-Cat were the dead father and his dead son, their bodies stiff with the cold.

George absently studied the tread pattern of the half-track Sno-Cat and thought. There were now sixteen deaths connected to this mysterious green fungus. No way to contact Sir Abner and the Consortium. He thought of what one of the troopers had told Baslovitch—young Morgan Mistral had heard something in the air. A helicopter? But few pilots would possess the combination of skill and foolhardiness or desperation to take a chopper up in this foul weather.

He shook his head. Baslovitch, himself a fine chopper pilot, would know that. Yet Baslovitch had whispered to him before boarding the Sno-Cat, "Must be a helicopter, George." Then Baslovitch had said nothing more.

George shook his head. He started over the drift, skidding, catching himself. He was getting good at it. Yellow light shone through the condensation that covered the glass in the double doors of the police station.

The right-hand door was opening, and he could see Tatiana—Louise—in the doorway. "Was everything all right?" she shouted over the keening of the wind.

"No, Louie, everything was all wrong," Baslovitch called back.

Baslovitch came over the snowdrift immediately after the two state troopers. George was the first one through the door, and the warmth of the police station's interior was immediately stifling. The air smelled sweet in a sickening sense, not pleasant at all. He started opening his parka.

"Where's the chief?" George heard Ralph ask.

"Dr. Holcomb called in on his CB radio. He'd received a message from his base station that Milly Perkins was having her baby. The doctor was stuck and couldn't get into town. I volunteered to go help, but the chief said he'd delivered babies in rainstorms, ice storms and everything else—a snowstorm wouldn't be much different. It's only about three blocks from here. He'll be back when he can."

George watched Baslovitch lean against the counter that served as the charge desk. "Morgan was dead," the former KGB man said. "And that green fungus George spoke of was all over the boy."

"My God," Tatiana whispered.

Baslovitch nodded. He was looking tired, George thought. "And then Andy..." Baslovitch hesitated.

"Shot himself," George whispered, his voice tight. "Dead."

Tatiana moved across the room, leaning her head against Baslovitch's left shoulder. "Who—"

"I don't know," Baslovitch whispered, folding her into his arms, turning his eyes up toward the ceiling.

George walked to the far end of the room, beside the frosted glass door with the word *Chief* on it. "There's not a damned thing we can do, not with this storm," he said.

Tatiana looked up from her husband's shoulder. "I made coffee, and I found a bottle of whiskey. The four of you need both." She started unzipping the front of her husband's ski parka.

12

The business in the bedroom had been most unsatisfying. And now Jilly Mason was stone-cold sober. He sat smoking a cigarette in the dining room of the rented house two blocks from the entrance to the factory. He waited for the Master of D.E.A.T.H. The Master reminded him very much of Johannes Krieger—the ruthlessness.

Mason had seen the elaborate spraying equipment at the factory when the Master had brought him there. He had seen similar equipment once, long ago. He had flown helicopters in Vietnam. He had been very good at it. And once he had flown specially equipped machines that had sprayed chemical defoliant across the canopy of the jungle.

This equipment was roughly the same, only more modern, more state of the art.

He knew what the Master had to be planning. "All those people," he murmured. He decided another drink was in order, and he stood up and walked across the room to the small bar. He took down a bottle of gin and half-filled a whiskey tumbler.

He heard the door into the dining room open and he looked toward it, downing half the contents of the glass. It was the Master. "Hello, how are you?" Mason said cordially.

"Excellent, Mr. Mason. You are admirably prompt. Things went well for you?"

"Yes," Mason lied. Things had not gone well at all. He would not let the boy be killed; he would figure some way out of that. "Yes, I want to thank you very much."

"Your skill has rewarded me enough. Our testing is nearly complete. And I wish you to assist in the conduct of the last phase before we move on to greater things." The Master's face contorted into a smile, but Jilly Mason thought the eyes were still very dead and penetrating.

He decided to dazzle the Master with brilliance. "The spraying equipment I saw at the factory—we're going to do a city, aren't we?"

The Master laughed. "First things first. You can spray a city for me if you like. But before that, another task."

"Certainly. What is it?"

"There are certain men who are involved in a very special operation on my behalf even as we speak. When the operation is concluded, they will walk out to a specific spot and then send a radio signal that will be relayed to the factory. And then I wish for you to go out and pick them up. The flying conditions may be very terrible. But it will be necessary for you to do this."

"Certainly. When should I leave?"

"It may be a matter of a few hours or less. It may be considerably longer. Much depends on the operation and its success. So you had better get some rest. I suggest you use your own room."

Jilly Mason nodded, slugging away the remainder of the gin in his glass. "Again, I'd like to thank you for having me rescued from that horrible prison."

"Your qualifications, your background, that is what saved you from that place. There is no need to thank me, Mr. Mason."

Jilly Mason had earlier decided the Master of D.E.A.T.H. was insane. But he had worked for crazy people before. Experience was a marvelous teacher.

13

They had made love there on the couch, and afterward he had carried her into the bedroom on the mezzanine-like second floor of the A frame and undressed her. They had showered together, washing each other's bodies, then made love again in the shower.

Dan Track looked at the digital clock beside the bed, faintly seeing the gleaming electroless nickel finish of the Scorpion beside it. It was twelve-thirty.

"I can't sleep, can you?" Desiree Goth's voice whispered from the darkness.

"No, I can't."

She moved nearer and one of her hands played with the hair on his chest. "Why don't you set the clock and we can get up before dawn tomorrow. I can make turkey sandwiches. You wouldn't mind turkey sandwiches for breakfast, would you?"

"No, it sounds good."

"I can make a thermos of coffee and we can ski through the pass and then climb to the east crest and watch the sunrise."

"I love you," he whispered, and he leaned over to the clock and set the alarm.

IT WOULD BE COLD, and Track dressed accordingly: thin, thermal-insulated underwear, a wind shirt, the warmest of the ski gear he had. He had filled his hip flask with Myers's Dark Rum just in case something more than coffee would be needed and, because of the conditions, packed the Thermos sportsman's blanket. If either of them were injured during the climb—he didn't worry about the skiing because objectively he knew both he and Desiree to be very good skiers—warmth would be critical. He secured the bib front of the insulated overall-like ski pants. He was tempted not to take a gun; somehow it would be a reminder that once the storm abated they would be leaving this place. But years of remaining alive because he had carried a gun overcame sentiment and he walked to the bedside table.

In the drawer of the nightstand was the Metalife Custom L-Frame .357. He closed the drawer, wanting something more compact, like the Trapper Scorpion .45. Unless he wanted to borrow Desiree's little Model 60 Smith. He shrugged. It would be the Scorpion.

He walked to the closet and reached to the top shelf for his flight bag, pulled it down and opened it. He had been trying the Special Weapons Badger shoulder holster. It was of fabric rather than leather, and he had made the decision to try the holster because fabric gear was the thing of the future—at least to some extent. He had found the rig comfortable. He held up the shoulder holster. On the right side was a double magazine pouch. In each of the compartments was a Detonics 8-round magazine that would hang out the butt of the Scorpion but functioned perfectly with it. Clipped behind and between the magazines in an upside-down carry was his Gerber MkI boot knife. He slipped the rig across his shoulders, going back to the nightstand for the Scorpion. He buttoned out the magazine and cycled the slide—the chamber was empty, a far safer way to engage in strenuous activity such as skiing or climbing. Track shoved the cut-down 6-round magazine back up the well and secured the pistol in the holster under his armpit.

It was very concealable, but concealment didn't really matter under the circumstances.

He walked from the room, Desiree waiting for him. "Men complain about women taking—"

She stopped.

Track smiled, gesturing to the gun, "Well?"

She started to laugh. "My revolver and a speed-loader are in my backpack."

"And you talk about me," he said.

He helped her into the hooded, heavily insulated, fur-trimmed parka. It was deep maroon, like the ski pants she wore. Beneath the parka she wore a gray turtleneck sweater that showed at her throat as she zipped the parka closed. Track shouldered into the navy blue parka, which matched his pants, then helped Desiree with her day pack.

"You got the sandwiches and the coffee?"

"*You've* got the sandwiches and the coffee." She smiled.

"Is that why my pack's so heavy?"

"I made a lot of sandwiches." As they started together for the door he glanced at the face of his Rolex. In a little more than an hour, it would be dawn. There was plenty of time.

14

The snow tractor's heating system was on one notch short of full blast and it was still cold inside. Chesterton worked the wheel, guiding the vehicle around a ridge of snow. Beside him, Zulu asked, "Would you like me to do some of the driving, Sir Abner?"

"No—thanks anyway, Zulu, but driving is the only way to keep my feet from freezing and falling off. But thank you very much."

"I make it another hour or better before we reach the house."

"Too bad," Chesterton mused, "that there wasn't a safe drop zone somewhere nearer."

"Too many cliffs. The terrain too unpredictable. But we should be there before Desiree and Major Track awaken."

"If Hudson hasn't gotten there first."

Zulu didn't answer.

Chesterton decided to make conversation, any kind of exercise would help to keep him warm. "Tell me, Zulu, why do you insist on calling Dan 'Major' all the time?"

"It irritates him, so I enjoy it," Zulu replied evenly. Chesterton turned to stare at Zulu, then looked back through the partially frosted flat windshield. "I thought you realized," Zulu added.

"To irritate the man?"

"I have a great deal of respect for Major Track, Sir Abner. And I like him, oddly enough. But I dislike the prospect of his knowing that. Consequently, I use the military title he eschews in his civilian life as a means of preventing his knowing that I like him. He is as certain of the respect, as I am certain of his. Devilishly clever of me, don't you think?"

"Clever? You must be joking, old man!"

"Consider, Sir Abner. The major first came into my life when he tried, unsuccessfully of course, to arrest Desiree—"

"But that was years ago," Chesterton interrupted.

"The first interaction between the major and myself was my bludgeoning him across the head with the barrel of a shotgun. Not the ideal way to begin a relationship."

"But I'll say it again, old man—that was years ago!"

"First impressions are lasting impressions, Sir Abner, as we all know. The major has always been the major to me, and he always will be. Take yourself, for example. On repeated occasions I have heard you insist that the major call you by your first name only, rather than preceding it with your title."

"Of course, and I wish you would, as well."

"But my first impression of you was an impression of a gentleman. Calling you Sir Abner fits so much more neatly. And so you shall always be Sir Abner to me and to Major Track."

"You're a very odd man, Zulu," Chesterton observed, and he laughed. "Perhaps I should start calling you Mr. Zulu."

"I shouldn't think so, Sir Abner. I am Zulu. I have been only Zulu for what seems too long a time to remember. When the last of my family died—" Zulu's voice sounded slightly strained "—my wife...when she died, the last word she spoke was my true name. And no one has spoken it since. Not even I. I am Zulu now, and forever.''

Chesterton didn't know what to say, and so he just kept driving.

STONE HUDSON BROUGHT the armored Zeiss binoculars to his eyes, focusing on the large, snow-covered A frame visible to him at the valley's edge in the gray light immediately prior to dawn. The snow still fell in large flakes and he was very cold. But he was satisfied. Smoke rose from a chimney near the back of the house. When he had arranged for the telephone lines into the entire district to be sabotaged, he had elected not to disrupt electrical power. There was no use bringing meaningless hardship to others not directly concerned in what he had to do, nor for that matter meaningless hardship to Major Track and the woman, Desiree Goth.

He imagined Track and Desiree Goth snug in their bed. As he scanned the house with the binoculars, he muttered, "Hope you humped her good, buddy. It was your last chance."

Hudson looked at his watch. The sweep second hand was rising to the top of the face; another minute gone— for Track, for Desiree Goth. In five more minutes, the attack would begin.

He watched the house, just to make sure.

THEY HAD LEFT their skis and poles and started climbing. It wasn't really hazardous, just tiring. Their first morning at the house in the mountains above Twisted Oak, Idaho, they had climbed to the top of the mountain along the overlook and watched the sunrise. And so it seemed fitting to repeat the adventure on their last morning.

At the midway point they had stopped, Desiree getting the thermos from Track's pack and pouring them a cup of coffee to share. The coffee cooled almost as soon as it was poured. But it had warmed him a little, at least he had convinced himself that it had. Then they had resumed the climb.

They were at the top of the overlook now, and Track folded his arm around Desiree's shoulders. "The trick—" she laughed "—is not to think about being cold. Think about something else."

"Okay, I'll think about being numb," Track suggested brightly.

"You're incorrigible."

"Probably," Track agreed. He started walking with her then, toward the overlook. He curled his wrist upward along her left shoulder, using the friction of her jacket against his arm to roll back the storm sleeve on his parka sufficiently to view the face of the Rolex. If the calendar on the kitchen wall was correct, sunrise would be in four minutes.

They kept walking. The wind was calmer at the higher elevation, and some of the effect of the cold had diminished.

They reached the edge of the overlook, standing not too close to it because with the drifting of the snow, it was impossible to tell exactly where the rock edge ended and the false edge sculpted in snow began.

To one side, he could see the house they had shared these past weeks—the place would always be special to him. He had been considering contacting the rental agent and inquiring if the house could be purchased. It was remote, but sometimes remote was very nice. It would be a good place to go with Desiree, to be with her.

He looked at her. "I love you very much, you know that?"

She leaned her head against his chest.

The pines in the lower elevations were still cloaked in darkness, highlighted sporadically by the snow that clung heavily to their boughs. Portions of the valley were still shrouded in night. A gray light washed the rest.

He looked at the Rolex again. It was nearly time for sunrise. Together, they turned to face the east, waiting.

Suddenly, he heard a sound he recognized instantly. He had heard it many times before. The woosh of a LAW rocket. He heard it a second time, and he turned toward the house. An explosion was followed by a second and a third. Flames were licking skyward from both sides of the house and from the rear of the house. Desiree pushed close against him. "Dan! What—"

"Shh," he whispered, holding her tightly to him.

More rockets were fired, the explosions deafening on the cold predawn air. The long, heavy, unpleasant sounds of machine guns followed, and the sounds tore through the cold as Desiree buried her head into his jacket.

"Our house," she screamed over the cacophony of gunfire and the roar of flames.

Track turned away from the house, forcing her to turn away, as well. He lifted her chin with his gloved hand and together they watched the sunrise. He wondered if it might be the last time.

STONE HUDSON WALKED SLOWLY. Despite the cold, despite the desire to be near the heat of the burning house, he trusted the efficiency of Major Track. And he trusted the efficiency of the woman, too. If one or both of them was still alive in the house—part of it toward the rear did not burn because the direction of the wind was wrong—there would be a weapon trained on him.

"This is Hudson!" he shouted. "If either one of you is alive in there, put a bullet into your head now and save me the trouble!"

There was no answer from the house. He shouted to Greenwald. "Get one of the machine guns and come with me."

Hudson started around in a wide arc toward the rear of the house, seeing Greenwald coming with the M-60, a link belt draped over his chest and shoulder. "Take it easy, Greenwald. If those people are alive in there, they're tough, and they know they're gonna die. Hit the second-floor window—it's the bedroom."

He stopped at the rear of the house, and Greenwald halted beside him. The M-60 came to life, what was left of the shattered glass doors that led to the small balcony blowing inward. "Do it good, Greenwald!" he shouted.

The MG kept firing for another thirty seconds, and then Hudson shouted, "That's enough. Cover me, I'm goin' up!" Hudson started ahead, the M-16 tensioned against his right shoulder on its sling, the pistol grip in his right fist. A narrow, wooden staircase led from the ground floor, built against the incline of the valley. He tested the steps first, then began to ascend.

He reached the small balcony, kicked out a remaining large shard of thermopane glass and stepped through.

Everything in the room that could be broken was broken.

The bed was made.

Track and the woman weren't there.

He had missed them.

He moved to the nightstand on the far side of the bed and picked up a copy of *Vogue* magazine. As he crossed the room around the bottom of the bed, his boots crunched over broken pieces of glass and plastic and metal. He reached the opposite nightstand. Brushing off the shattered remains of a digital clock, he pulled open a drawer and lifted out a revolver. A Smith & Wesson L-Frame. It was heavily customized, the 4-inch barrel slab-sided like a PPC revolver, the rear sight-blade rounded. He could tell from the weight that it was loaded. On the left barrel flat it read in gold-filled engraving, Metalife Custom, Reno, Pa.

On the right barrel flat, in gold-filled engraving again, Dan Track.

Hudson set down the revolver on the bed, unzipped his parka and stuffed the revolver into his waistband. In the drawer where it had been were three loaded Safariland speedloaders. He pocketed these, as well.

He crossed the room to the closet, kicking open the sliding door, shattering it. He fired a burst from the M-16 through the opening just in case they were hiding inside.

He looked in—clothes, mostly women's clothes, some men's clothing. In the far corner was what he was looking for. A SPAS-12 shotgun, the stock folded, the smoothbore leaning up from the massive pistol grip. He gathered it up, slinging it across his back. A musette-like bag was beside it, and he opened it to discover double O buck loads and slug loads for the shotgun. Two more speedloaders for the revolver, a box of .45 ACP Federal 185-grainers, a box of .357 Federal 158-grain soft points, a lockblade Puma folding knife, and a Milt Sparks Six-Pack with six loaded Colt magazines occupied a second, identical bag. He took both bags and started back across the room, through the shot-out glass doors and into the wind again.

He shouted down to Greenwald. "Tell the guys to get ready to torch this place. I want it burned to the ground. Track and the woman are gone, probably on skis. If Track's anywhere nearby he'll have heard us. All he should have on him is that little .45 of his. Most he could have would be two spare magazines. The woman probably has her damned revolver. I want that Travel-all by the side of the house made so it won't run again no matter what anybody does to it. Get on the radio to McCormick. Tell him to get the guys up here with the snowmobiles right away. Track and the woman can't be far. We're goin' after them.''

''Right, Colonel.''

Greenwald started off through the snow at a jog trot and Hudson descended the steps.

The little .45 Track carried had a 6-round magazine, maybe one extra in the chamber. Even if Track used an extension magazine, he wouldn't have more than a spare sixteen rounds on him. And at anything but close range, the woman's pistol would be useless. Maybe a knife. Hudson shrugged.

If the cold didn't get them, he would.

And he didn't want the cold to get them.

15

They had climbed down from the overlook in relative silence. As they affixed the bindings of their skis, Track spoke. "I made seven of them. At least from the gunfire and the rockets."

"I agree," Desiree answered. Her voice was one of resignation, of defeat.

"Probably got some backup—either a helicopter coming for them or they've got snowmobiles or arctic cats somewhere out there. Other people with those if they do."

"They may think we died in the house," Desiree said.

"I don't think so. It's probably Hudson and his men. Hudson would check. It didn't look as though the back of the house had caught. If they got up there, they'd know I left my shotgun and my revolver. They'll know we didn't leave in a hurry, and they'll be after us."

"Twisted Oak?" she asked.

"No. It's closest, but if we head for Twisted Oak, they might have people out there to cut us off or stop us when we get there. We've still got the sandwiches—if we keep moving and pace ourselves, we can head off in the opposite direction toward the counties along the Montana border. If the snow keeps falling, they won't find our ski tracks."

"If we can route ourselves, we can do most of it downhill."

"And make some time," Track agreed. "Save the sandwiches for tonight, and the coffee, too."

"There are a lot of little towns out there."

"Yeah," Track agreed. He had drawn the Scorpion from the Special Weapons rig, and he was jacking back the slide. He upped the safety and started to reholster the gun. But he stopped and looked at her. "I'm sorry, Desiree. I'm sorry for the house being destroyed. For everything. I really am."

"Not for everything. Never be sorry for everything."

"You know what I mean," he told her softly.

"And you know what I mean. I spent my whole life making money, evading the law, all of that. And I spent my whole life not trusting anybody except Zulu. And then I met you. I wouldn't change that. If I die today, I wouldn't change any moment with you."

She pulled her maroon ski toque down over her face so only her eyes showed. They were beautiful, Track thought, looking at her. She pulled the goggles down over the opening for the eyes, and then pulled the hood up.

Track pulled down his own toque, put his goggles in place, then upped his hood.

"I'm ready," he heard her say.

Track nodded, then dug in his poles.

16

It had taken two hours to find the problem in the electrical system of the half-track and after that ten minutes for Zulu to fix it. Chesterton had driven as quickly as he could but it had been almost 10:00 A.M. local time before they had reached the valley.

He sat in the half-track now, staring. He had seen a photograph of the house when he had helped arrange the rental. A luxurious A frame hideaway with glass all around.

Now it was a smoking ruin, a few twisted pieces of metal. "We're too late, Zulu," Chesterton began. But then he couldn't speak anymore.

He looked at Zulu.

Tears rimmed the African's eyes. "We shall search the ruins for some clue."

"They can't have survived that."

"All the same, we'll search the ruins, look for the remains of their bodies. If we find none, then Sir Abner, we shall search out there until we do."

Chesterton felt a shiver along his spine. "Of course we will, I wasn't thinking. Dan would have gotten her out somehow."

"Yes, the major would have tried. And if we find them and they are dead, then I shall do to Hudson what I did to the men who murdered my wife, my children and my parents. I trailed them through the jungle. It took many days."

"Don't, my friend."

"I will tell you, so you will know. I crept up on them in the night, and killed them with my knife. All but the leader. He was the one who had ordered their deaths. I disarmed the man and I put down my weapons. We fought. The fight lasted for a little better than two hours. He was very strong. A very good fighter. I could have killed him several times, but I did not. I slowly beat him to death, and then I ripped him apart—quite literally limb from limb. I buried each of the parts in a different place so his spirit would not find peace. If this Hudson has caused the death of Desiree, I shall do this to him, and you, my friend, you shall not stop me."

Slowly, evenly, Chesterton said to his friend, "I will join you, Zulu, I swear that I will join you," and he clapped the man's shoulder and together they stared through the breath-frosted glass of the half-track.

17

George Beegh opened his eyes. He had an aversion to sleeping in jail cells and so he had spread his sleeping bag across the floor of the police station's outer office and spent the night that way. He was the first one to fall asleep and the last one to awaken, he realized. The sleeping bags Baslovitch had taken from the Mistrals' General Merchandise Store for himself and Tatiana to sleep in were rolled neatly and on the charge desk. Ralph and Harry had slept in shifts in the cell. George guessed if you were a cop, sleeping in a cell didn't bother you.

He looked across the room at Harry, who sat by the radio. "Hi. There a world still out there?"

"Yeah, sure is. I just picked up a weird transmission flippin' through the shortwave bands here. Some guys out in this weather huntin' or somethin'—crazy."

George sat up, scratching the stubble on his chin. "What was it?"

Harry wheeled around in his swivel chair and held up a pad of paper. The neat uniform appearance was gone: hair rumpled, shirt wrinkled, collar open. "Damnedest thing. I copied it down." Harry cleared his throat. "'Hudson to Pursuit Two. Converge on Fat Woman's Creek. Repeat. Converge on Fat Woman's Creek. Got a blood trail. Following track. Hudson out.'"

George sat up, nearly tripping because his shoeless feet were still inside the bag. He kicked out of the sleeping bag and was beside Harry in three strides. "Let me see that." He read the message, then read it again. "You sure this Hudson guy didn't say 'tracks'?"

"Coulda. What have I got here?" Harry peered at the pad. "I guess he said track."

"No," George whispered. "He didn't say track. He said *Track*." George found his cigarettes and lit a Winston. He inhaled the smoke deep into his lungs. "Harry," George whispered. "Harry—you monitor that band. Don't get off it."

"But—"

"Just do it, Harry. See if you can get some kind of fix on them."

"Hell," Harry said. "Don't need a fix. I know where Fat Woman's Creek is. It used to be a town. Ghost town now, though—just like they have in the Southwest. There was a mining operation up there around the turn of the century. It faded out and everybody left. About seventy miles from here. Maybe seventy-five."

"Anybody flyin'?"

"What?"

"I mean a police chopper or anything."

"No. Snow is comin' down as hard as ever. Look out the window."

George nodded. "Where's everybody—like Peter and Louise and—"

"Ralph and them's across the street, over at Sandy's. Hey—" George was into one boot and working on the other "—bring me back a cup of coffee, huh? That Louise, she makes good coffee, but Sandy's, I don't know—got a different taste to it."

George nodded. "Yeah, cleaning fluid."

Both boots on, he stomped his feet a few times on the floor to settle in, then grabbed his shoulder holster for the Smith 469, slinging it on over his sweater. He found his .45 on the floor next to where he had slept and worked the slide to chamber a round, then upped the safety and stuffed it in the Bianchi rig that was still on his belt. He pulled on his coat and his Jack Daniel's baseball cap as he started through the door, saying, "I won't forget the coffee, just listen for any transmissions like I said, Harry," and he slammed the door shut. George was instantly freezing. But he clambered over the snowbank—and passed the Sno-Cat parked where they had left it. When they had returned, they had moved the bodies of Morgan and Andy Mistral to the local undertaker's with the injunction that neither body be touched.

George half ran, half skated across the main street toward the café. No traffic moved. A strong wind blew. Snow fell in huge flakes. George glanced at his Rolex. It was a little after ten. They had let him sleep too late.

He reached the opposite snowbank and started up, holding on to the top of a No Parking sign for support and then skating down the opposite side, nearly losing his balance on the sidewalk. He skated, ran ahead along the snow-packed and ice-slicked sidewalk. Past a newspaper office that also sold stationery and photographic supplies. Past the Christian bookstore.

At the café, George wrenched open the right-hand door, wiping his feet on the mat as he drew the door closed behind him.

He could see Baslovitch, Tatiana and Ralph at the counter. George almost called out "Sergei," but he caught himself in time. "Peter! Harry intercepted a message on the shortwave band. Hudson's up here, and somehow Dan is here, too—I don't know why. Maybe Sir Abner sent him in. Last I knew he was on vacation someplace with Desiree."

"Hudson?" Baslovitch wheeled on his stool.

"He works for the Master of D.E.A.T.H. Hudson's men are the ones who paralyzed Ellen, the girl I told you about. He's a killer. A madman. And he's tracking Dan about seventy miles from here."

George stopped in the middle of the floor. Sandy, the woman who ran the café, dropped a cup of coffee behind the counter. He heard her mutter, "Shit!"

Sergei Baslovitch stood up quickly. "We can take extra fuel for the Sno-Cat." And Baslovitch turned to his wife. "Darling, get the Cat fueled. Get all the extra containers you can find and fill them up. We may need quite a lot."

"What the hell is going on? 'Master of D.E.A.T.H.'?" Ralph asked.

George and Baslovitch looked at Ralph. Baslovitch said, "Not a nice person, Ralph. Not a nice person at all. Ralph, you give George and me a hand. We'll have to rob Andy Mistral's store of food, a tent, perhaps some extra clothing—"

"More ammo," George noted. "But wait a minute," and he turned to Sandy, still behind the counter. "Men's room?" he asked.

She didn't say anything, just pointed to the far back of the restaurant and George saw a swinging wooden door with two silhouetted faces on it, one male and one female.

"Thank you." George started off to do what he had to do.

He could hear Baslovitch talking to Ralph while he crossed the room. "You'll have to pinpoint this area for me on a topographic map. George can catch up to us—come on."

"Master of D.E.A.T.H.?" Ralph asked again.

As George let the door swing closed behind him, he heard Tatiana, her voice sounding lifeless, say, "Yes, Master of D.E.A.T.H., Ralph."

18

Dan Track cursed his stupidity. "You leave me here," he hissed through his chattering teeth to Desiree Goth.

"No, and you can't make me. What are you going to do? There's not a thing you can do to make me, so let me see it."

He nodded, too tired to argue with her. "I'm going to have to cut your pant leg," she said.

"You're just looking for a cheap thrill," Track told her, trying to make her laugh.

"Do you have anything besides that Gerber MkI?"

"Yeah." Track nodded. He started fishing in the outside pocket of his jacket for the Swiss army knife. It was a Victorinox, a good one. "Here," and he handed it to her. "Don't break a nail on it and holler at me."

"I won't."

Track's left leg hurt when she moved it. Bullet wounds usually did, he reflected. Through his teeth—he didn't know if they chattered because of the cold or because of the pain—he said, "I think the bullet went right through."

"Just like in your American westerns." She laughed. "A flesh wound? I hope you're right."

They had skied for more than two hours before stopping. And while they were resting, Track heard the sound. A snowmobile. He climbed up onto the snow-covered rocks, Desiree behind him holding their skis and their gear. And they waited. When the snowmobile passed beneath them, Track leaped from the rocks and attacked both men. He killed the driver instantly with his knife. The second man drew a pistol and Track lunged at him. All the while the snowmobile was out of control and heading into the rocks. The pistol discharged and Track rammed the knife into the man's neck at the carotid artery, then jumped clear of the snowmobile.

When he tried to stand up, he realized he had been shot. He tried to walk, but fell down, and the snow stained red with his blood. The snowmobile went into the rocks and bounced over the edge of a cliff, taking both men and their weapons with it.

"I really fucked up," he told Desiree. They sure could have used that snowmobile.

"No you didn't." She nearly had the seam cut. "I'm cutting it this way so I can use the sewing kit in my pack and stitch your trousers back together. You'll get frost-bitten if I don't. And you have pretty legs."

Track tried to laugh—he didn't want to.

"Look at it this way," Desiree told him. "You killed two—that's two less. Maybe it will slow up the others a little."

"Not half as slow as I'll be. You leave me here. Give me your little .38. Take the .45 and try to get help."

"Bullshit," Desiree Goth muttered. "You know I don't like shooting a .45 that much."

"Do as I say."

"Just because you tell me you love me and ask me to marry you, I should suddenly do as you say?"

"Dammit!"

"I thought men like you were supposed to be so stoic."

"That's just a lot of movie bullshit. Really tough men wince at the slightest—PAIN!"

"Talk to me," she said, "while I explore the wound."

"Look, you wouldn't like exploring the wound, really—"

"I have to make sure the bullet is out. I'm experienced with bullet wounds. You can't be in my business and not get experienced with them. Rather like somebody who sells cars never seeing a wreck, you know. Talk to me. Tell me how beautiful I am. Or how beautiful you are."

And she started to probe the wound. Track sucked in his breath.

"Talk to me," she insisted.

"Okay," he gasped. "Okay. If you leave me—"

"Talk about something else or your leg will really hurt."

"Okay, you really make a great turkey. My sister, she was a good cook when we—aww shit—when we had the money to—to buy a turkey! Dammit, that—"

"That hurts. You're lucky."

"I'm lucky it hurts?"

"No," she answered, her voice soft, even, low. "No, you're lucky that it is just a flesh wound. But you have lost some blood."

"No shit, I could have told you that. I'm sorry," Track said through his teeth.

"I think he was using 9mm solids. The gun he had looked like a Hi-Power."

"Well, I'm sure glad he chose a good gun. Hate to—"

"This will hurt. I'm going to put some antiseptic on it. Good thing you brought the little first-aid kit."

"Yeah, lucky me," Track said with an attempt at a grin. "Tell me when you're going to—"

"Here, chew on my glove so you don't bite your tongue off or something."

"Chew on your glove. That's a little kinky, isn't it?"

"Hmm. With your leg hurt, when we make love I'll have to go on top of you. Do you think that's kinky?"

"Shut up. I can't handle the thought of that and the pain in my leg at the same time."

"Chew on the glove, now!"

He bit down hard on her glove.

"I'll talk to you," she said. He didn't watch what she was doing to his leg, but it was more than putting on a little antiseptic. "I think that if we take it easy, you should be able to ski. We'll have to watch what kinds of slopes we take. You showed me the map before we spotted the snowmobile. There was a town a few miles from here, wasn't there? Just nod."

Track nodded, his eyes shut against the pain.

"All right. We can get medical help there."

Track shook his head.

"Why not?"

Through the glove he rasped, "Ghost town."

"What?"

"Ghost town!" And he spit out the glove. "Nobody lives there. A town where nobody lives. Fat Woman's Creek. It was a mining town around the turn of the— aww Jesus, that hurts."

"I'm about finished."

"You and me both," Track said.

"Tell me about the ghost town."

Track nodded, leaning his head back, snowflakes falling across his eyelashes as he looked skyward. "I read about it. Before all the snow started a few days ago I'd thought maybe we could drive over there, spend the day...you know. Kind of give you a—aagh!"

"I'm sorry. Give me a what?" she asked.

Through gritted teeth, he said, "A shot of Americana. The mine just played out and everybody left. The buildings are still standing. Got a saloon, a hotel, a brothel—"

"Sounds wonderful. Take your girl to a brothel for a holiday, hmm?"

"You almost done?"

"Almost," she said, smiling. Track looked at her, then looked away. "Men are such babies," she said.

"Fine, you get shot in the leg sometime and let's see how good it feels to you!"

"There, I had to make the bandage tight enough to hold but not so tight as to cut off circulation."

"Florence Nightingale strikes again."

"Can you stand?" she asked him.

"Give me a minute."

"You shouldn't have skied down from the rocks with me. We should have fixed your leg up there. You lost too much blood."

"Look," he told her. "Hudson and his guys will have found their dead pals by now. They're probably ten minutes behind us, Hudson and the rest of them."

"Downhilling it we've got a chance, even against their snowmobiles. And the snow is still covering our tracks. This ghost town place is perfect, they would never think—"

"We'd be stupid enough to go there," Track finished for her.

"All right, if you want to put it that way."

"Help me up," Track told her.

"Put your arm around my shoulders," she responded.

He did and she helped him to his feet. Through his teeth—his leg hurt like a bad tooth now—he told her, "Talk to me in French—you know how I love it."

"*Merde à vous,*" she said.

"That wasn't a nice thing to say." He was standing, but not too well.

"Try to stand on your own. Here," and she gave him his ski poles. He put both of them into his left hand awkwardly and leaned, taking some of the pressure off his leg. "I need to move your left leg a little so I can get the ski back on."

Track nodded, licking his lips and thought about the business of skiing to the ghost town. He wasn't going to make it. He knew that. But he also knew that if he didn't, she would stay with him. And there wasn't any way to force her to do otherwise, so he had to make it. He started giving himself a pep talk. One of the buildings in Fat Woman's Creek would probably have some old furniture in it, or maybe even some firewood. After eighty years or better, it would be so dry it would burn like crazy. A fire would be good. Warmth. He could have a sip of the rum from his pack, or was it in her pack?

No fire, he realized.

"Aagh." It really hurt when he had to stand on his left leg while she had moved his right foot into his other ski.

If they lit a fire, Hudson and his men might see it. If he and Desiree made it to the town, maybe he could talk her into leaving him there and going for help. He doubted his luck but it would be worth a try. The next nearest town was about seventy-five miles from there. That could take her days, alone on skis. And what if Hudson's men spotted her trail? He started to rethink the logic of getting her away from him—to safety, or to her death?

"There," she said. "Good practice for me so I can help you with your slippers. All set." She stood up, smiled at him and asked, "Do you think we can try it now?"

"Yeah, I guess. You know somethin'?"

"What?"

"You're a hell of a tough person, kid."

She leaned up to him and kissed him hard on the mouth. "You first," she said, pulling her toque down, then reaching up and pulling down his. She moved his goggles down into position, then set about closing his jacket for him. She pulled her own goggles down, then upped her hood. "I'll be right behind you," she told him, her eyes smiling through the goggles.

Track nodded. He dug in his poles and tried to edge forward a little. His left leg screamed at him to immediately stop such foolishness. He tried to ignore it. He tried picturing Desiree naked in his mind; if he could get his mind off of the pain, the leg would function better, he knew.

She was so tall and so—he couldn't think of a word, but he could picture the slight fullness at her hips, the flatness of her stomach.

He kept moving, picking up a little speed. He found that if he avoided twisting the leg inward, it worked better.

She had whipstitched his pant leg together but he could still feel the cold air. It helped to numb the wound and he told himself that was good.

The terrain dipped suddenly, and Dan Track launched himself ahead, shouting to Desiree, "God, this hurts!"

He looked back; she was right behind him.

19

George Beegh stood behind the counter at the late Andy Mistral's General Merchandise Store, loading one backpack with shotgun shells—all twelve gauges, mixing double O buck and slug loads, disregarding the boxes, casting them aside. He had already loaded the first of the backpacks with 9mm and .45 ACP. He finished with the shot shells and zipped the pack closed across the top. It was a day pack and would be hell to carry with such weight.

In the background, as he turned away from the counter and started hauling the two packs to the front doors, he could hear Baslovitch trying the actions on shotguns. "I'll take this Remington and this Mossberg."

"Find us a bolt action with a good set of iron sights. There won't be any time to try messing with a scope that isn't zeroed."

"Where's a Steyr-Mannlicher SSG when you could really use one, huh? Ahh...wait a minute. I've used one of these before."

George looked over his shoulder. "What?"

"This is a pre-64—my God. Winchester makes a good rifle—you know?"

"Grab some ammo for it," George told him, setting down one of the packs and opening the door onto the street. He started through, lifting both packs again. The

Sno-Cat was already running. Tatiana stuck her head out on the passenger side. "Give you a hand?"

"No, I'm fine."

"I got the heat in this thing working. It was a bad thermostat. I put in a new one."

"Scientists," George said.

Tatiana whispered, "Shh...housewife now. That's all."

George nodded, swinging in first one pack, then the other. Tatiana had edged back and started dragging one of the packs rearward. "You let me do that," George told her, but she was already almost to the back of the vehicle with it.

"You take care of my husband. I still think I should come along."

He heard Baslovitch's voice behind him. "No, you shouldn't."

"Spoilsport!"

George shook his head.

"You ever been there—this Fat Woman's Creek place?" George asked him.

"No," Baslovitch answered, cutting the wheel on the Cat to avoid a ridge of snow built by the wind. In the afternoon the wind had increased as had the snowfall. "But I had Ralph and Harry mark the map. The terrain features should seem considerably different. You are very fortunate, I've taken survival courses in Siberia. Though in Siberia I don't think it snows as much."

"What do you think they meant by a blood trail?" George asked. "One of them's wounded?"

"You answered your own question, I think, George. Hopefully, it isn't a serious wound. My wife packed a medical kit. She got the materials from the doctor's office. Harry helped her break in."

"That woman ever have her baby yet? The one the police chief went to help?"

"No, I don't think so. Your uncle is a very tough man—and Desiree Goth is a very tough lady. If she's with him."

George wanted to change the subject. He lit a cigarette and saw that his hands were shaking. He put it down to the cold. "How are you and Tatiana making out?"

Baslovitch laughed.

"Shit, I didn't mean it that way."

"You should not call her Tatiana, George. One slip, well—who knows who may owe some allegiance to the KGB?"

"She's a lovely woman. But I don't envy either of you, having to live in fear for the rest of your lives," George said slowly.

"We don't live in fear, George, because you can't live that way. I found that out the hard way. In fact, because we do hide from the KGB, we enjoy life more."

"I don't understand that," George told him frankly.

"It is very simple. Each morning when we waken, we know perfectly well that it could be the last day of our lives, so we enjoy it. I am working on a book, and after I get it finished, Sir Abner will help in getting it published. It tells the true story of the KGB, the good and the bad. There are men and women in the KGB who risk their lives daily for the welfare of the Soviet people. And there are other kinds of men. I am telling the story of both kinds. It will be published under a pseudonym, of course, and great care will be exercised in how the royalties are sent to me. And Tatiana has a chemistry workshop set up in our basement. She's working on an improved method for utilizing decaying plant matter to power generators that will make electricity. A far cry from the experiments in physical science she used to perform, but it keeps her mind active. We are happy.''

"I'm getting married. I told you that.''

"Yes. And the girl, she was crippled by this Hudson's men—and they work for the Master of D.E.A.T.H.''

"Yes.''

"You would do well to adopt the same philosophy. Leave the worrying to others who have nothing else with which to fill their lives. That does not mean to be foolhardy, or to resign yourself to things. I never leave the house without a gun. Every room in our house has a gun in it hidden somewhere or another. If the KGB comes for us, we won't die without making a good fight of it. But whether they come tomorrow or never at all, we live each day as if it was our last, and try to make it the best day possible.''

"Why don't you just write inspirational poetry?'' George laughed.

Baslovitch laughed, as well. "But do you see what I mean?''

George stared through the windshield. It was warm enough in the Sno-Cat that he had unzipped his coat, taken off his Jack Daniel's baseball cap. He thought about Ellen. "Yeah, I see what you mean. The doctors told us that maybe someday there'll be an operative procedure that might correct her problem, and she might walk again. But the chances of that happening are not very good.''

"But there is a chance. So you can look at it two ways. Either worry about each day waiting for such a procedure to be developed and become available to her, or you can make the best of each day you have together. Waiting for some long-expected good is really just as hard as anticipating some dreaded evil. They both make you live beyond today. And the hazard is that someday you may wake up and find you have wasted an entire lifetime.''

"It's my eyes," George said, inhaling on his cigarette. "Everybody wants to father me or mother me."

"Have I spoken out of turn?"

"No." George laughed. "No, you haven't." He stared ahead into the swirling snow. They had to cover at least another fifty miles, perhaps two hours more travel time with the heavy snow, perhaps longer. That his uncle was out there and that men were trying to kill him was something of which he was certain. For a while, at least, he rested his thoughts in the future: saving his uncle's life and getting Stone Hudson, whom George wanted dead very badly.

SIR ABNER CHESTERTON decided that he now knew what it must be like to freeze to death. Thirty hours ago, he had been sweltering in a tropical jungle, swatting mosquitos, fighting heat and fantasizing about the cold. He laughed to himself. He now fantasized about the high temperatures of the jungle. Humanity, he thought....

"Here, Sir Abner!"

Chesterton looked up from the snow. Behind him, Zulu was waving his arm high in the air, a shotgun held in it. Chesterton started running as best he could across the snow, the snow so deep that with each step he sank into it up to his thighs. He could hear Zulu's voice. "I have found tracks, snowmobiles! I have found tracks."

After checking through the burned house as best they could for human remains, Hudson and his men would be following Track and Desiree through the snow. He and Zulu had begun the arduous task of working ever-widening circles looking for some sort of a sign. Chesterton kept moving. Zulu shouted again. "The tracks lead off to the east."

Chesterton sagged to a stop, still some twenty yards from Zulu. He shouted through the swirling snow over the wailing of the wind, "Are you sure? What if Hudson and his men are just guessing, haven't followed any trail?"

"In either event," Zulu shouted, "we are that much closer to our goal. If we can intercept Major Track and Desiree before Hudson and his men do, then we can effect their rescue. If we find Hudson and his men before they find the major and Desiree, then we will kill them. Come, we should hurry now," and Zulu took off across the snow toward the tractor that was only faintly discernible a hundred yards west. Chesterton had no breath to reply. He started to move again, clutching his Walther MPK submachine gun.

20

The downhill slope had ended six hundred yards or so beyond the outskirts of the abandoned town, and they had moved along more slowly, more painfully. Track leaned his weight across Desiree's shoulders to spare the left leg that had started bleeding again. He hoped that the snow would not stop falling, would cover their tracks, cover the blood he had left.

In his right fist, his poles swinging from his left hand, he held the Trapper Scorpion, his thumb poised over the safety to drop it instantly. He had stuffed his ski glove into his jacket, and the silk glove was all that protected his skin from the wind and cold. And his hand was numbing. The Scorpion hung well in his hand, but he didn't delude himself that the handmade .45 that had started life as a Commander and changed to something radically different would be any match for assault rifles, subguns and LAW rockets. With the Smith K-Frame near sight and the accuracy Trapper had built into the pistol, he could reliably hit torso-sized targets at one hundred yards. But with their assault rifles, Hudson and his men could reliably kill at more than twice that distance.

He kept moving.

"I don't hear anything," Desiree began. He knew she was trying to cheer him up. "If they had picked up our trail, we'd hear their snowmobiles by now."

"Right," he agreed.

They reached the edge of the town, and were greeted by drifts as high as eight feet along the windward side of the main street. A sign hung half-down. It read Hotel San Francisco. "Sounds like a nice place," Track told her.

"Too cold for cockroaches, isn't it?"

"It's never too cold for cockroaches. I was reading an article once in a magazine that claimed that if there was a nuclear war, cockroaches would probably survive. The carapace—I think that's what you call it—holds up well under radioactivity."

"And snow and cold, too, thank you very much." She smiled up at him.

"Anyway, let's try the bar. I'll feel more at home there," he told her.

"All right, the saloon it is."

"And if the actual bar is still in there, it might give us a little added cover." Track kept moving. His eyes scanned both sides of the street. At the center of the town on the windward side of the street, drifts piled high beside it, was a faded sign: Prospector's Paradise.

"That must be the saloon," Desiree observed. "Such a place you're taking me. Do you think they'll let me in wearing slacks?"

"I never have any problems, and I wear slacks wherever I go," Track told her, trying to laugh, not making it. They started angling toward the saloon now, working their way slowly up the drift. The drift began to level off. "Stop a second—huh kid?" Track caught his breath and snowflakes clung to his eyelashes. He exhaled a long cloud of steam, looking back along the main street toward the slope. He thought he could hear something. It was paranoia, perhaps, but he couldn't afford the gamble. "Hurry, let's get inside." They reached the top of the drift and Desiree skidded down on her skis, nearly losing her balance. The wind heightened, and Track prayed that it would continue. He needed it to obliterate the long, deliberate tracks they had carved in the virgin snow of the main street, the pressure marks they had placed on the drift they had climbed. He edged downward, losing his balance with a sudden spasm of pain, keeping his pistol up, Desiree half catching him. He sagged to his right knee, his left leg straight. "Get me outa these skis," he told her, "and do it fast, kid." He rolled over with his back against the snow-crusted exterior wall of the saloon.

Desiree worked at his bindings. "I hear it, too," she said. "Snowmobiles."

"Could be imagination—mass hallucination—like that."

"Uh-huh, or it could be the cavalry coming to the rescue, just like in your western movies. It would go with the town."

"The cavalry," Track grunted, standing, his leg screaming at him with pain, "doesn't use snowmobiles." The sound was getting louder now—several distinct engine pulses. Desiree grabbed the skis, and Track hobbled toward the boarded-up door. He hoped the boards were as old as they looked. He threw his weight against them; the one on the bottom cracked. Track backed off, glancing toward the street, but the snowdrift was too high to see over. The sound was louder, though. Track threw his weight against the boards again, and one of them fell away.

"All right, if I start to scream, hit me," Track told her, and he stepped back, taking all his weight on his bad left leg, twisting half left and launching a double tae kwon-do kick against the boards and the door. The remaining boards splintered, the door ruptured inward.

Track fell to his knees, then forward. He still clutched the Scorpion tight in his right fist.

"Dan—"

"All right, help me up," he breathed, his breath steaming in the cold. But he was sweating.

He was to his feet, the pain something he could not ignore at all, something that screamed at him as he moved. He braced one arm over Desiree's shoulders and limped through the door.

A long shaft of gray light flooded the center of the room through the open doorway. "Get my flashlight— the middle compartment of my pack. Wrapped up in the Thermos blanket," he said to Desiree.

He felt her opening his pack. Track moved the pistol toward the shadows surrounding them like a talisman to ward off evil. Its medicine wouldn't be strong enough for the evil that was coming, he thought bitterly.

"I have it!"

"Give me it," Track rasped. He twisted the head on, his weight on his right foot. "Get over there. Be careful. Try to arrange the boards as best you can and pull the door closed—hurry!"

"All right."

Track kept the beam of light aimed away from the street, sweeping it over the boarded-up saloon—a few tables, one of them overturned, not round tables like the ones in saloons in western movies, but squared off. On the far right of the saloon was a long bar. It wasn't ornately carved mahogany, at least not that he could tell. But it looked heavy. A shattered mirror covered with dust and coated with cobwebs half covered the wall behind it.

Track could hear the sounds of Desiree trying to get the door closed, and the sounds of the snowmobiles. He kept the light on—brand-new Duracells were in it. He had light to waste at the moment. He wasn't worried about the effect of the cold on the batteries. He hadn't been running it in the cold and the flashlight was small enough to hold the entire body of it in his fist and warm it.

The door was closed, the gray light all but gone suddenly.

"Dan?"

"Let's get behind the bar," Track told her. He tried to move, but he fell forward, his left leg giving under him.

"Dan!"

"I'm all right," and Track pulled up his right knee keeping his left leg out straight. Desiree helped him stand. "Get me behind the bar, then get the skis and the poles. We might need them. Hurry."

He had wished a thousand times since sunrise and the assault on the house that he had had the foresight to pack the L-Frame, to bring along the Sparks Six Pack with the six spare magazines for his Scorpion. He smiled. He wished he had brought the SPAS-12. But a 10-pound riot shotgun wasn't the sort of thing you took along for a casual outing on the slopes with your best girl.

They rounded the corner of the bar, Track leaning heavily against it. "I can take care of myself now. Hurry up, get the skis and the poles—hurry." She left him, running back as he shone the Mini Mag-Lite onto the main portion of the saloon floor. She had the skis, the poles.

For the first time Dan Track noticed that the snowmobiles' engine noises had stopped.

"Hurry," he called to Desiree in a loud stage whisper.

She ran through the beam of his flashlight and toward him.

Track shone the light along the length of the bar and onto the floor. Nothing repulsive seemed in evidence.

He hobbled ahead, then stood at the center of the bar.

In a second Desiree was beside him.

"What will we do?"

"You get out your gun. Don't shoot unless I tell you. Now put your pack back on. We might have to get out of here quick."

She started getting out of her pack, Track helping her, the flashlight off now. He kept his eyes riveted on the doorway.

Why was there no sound of snowmobiles?

Track licked his lips. They were cracked from the cold.

His right fist tightened on the Scorpion.

Desiree had her gun, stuffing a Safariland speed-loader for it into the pocket of her jacket.

Track looked at his left trouser leg—it was drenched with blood. He didn't say anything to her about it. Instead, "Very carefully, take my flashlight and look for a back way out of here. If you can see outside, see what it looks like out there. Be careful and get back here quick." He helped Desiree back into the day pack.

If the snowmobiles had stopped, it didn't necessarily mean Hudson and his men had found tracks. The snow had been falling heavily and rapidly.

But it was wholly possible, likely in fact, that Hudson would order his men to search the buildings, and regardless of how artfully Desiree might have done it, the displaced boards and the broken doorjamb would betray their presence. Snow would have dripped off their clothing onto the floor of the saloon; it would be clear they were here.

Track licked his lips again. He was feeling light-headed from the loss of blood.

Desiree returned. "There is a back door, but it's boarded up. If we both throw our weight against it we should be able to break it through. I could see out a crack between the boards. There is a flat area of about a hundred yards, and then the ground drops off, it looks like another downhill.''

Track nodded. ''You help me down, then let's eat those turkey sandwiches—we'll need the energy. Come on,'' and Track balanced himself on the edge of the bar, Desiree taking his left arm and putting it around her shoulders. ''Ouch,'' he said.

''Why do men have to be so much bigger than women? It makes this sort of thing awkward.''

''Natural selection over the ages. The bigger men were more successful in combat, in hunting—hell, how do I know?'' and he was down.

''We'll take care of the leg first.''

''Oh...we will, huh?'' But he nodded. She took his Swiss army knife from her parka pocket and sliced the whipstitching along the seam of his trouser by the outside flat of his left thigh. Track shook his head. ''That looks bad.''

''It's just that all the blood is smeared around it. I'll clean it, but be as quiet as you can.''

Track nodded. This time he took his own glove and bit down on it hard.

He focused his mind elsewhere. Likely his Metalife Custom L-Frame had been destroyed when the house had been destroyed, or stolen. He would miss it. It had been the most accurate revolver he had ever owned. He would ask his pal Ron Mahovsky to build him a new one, but it would never be quite the same. That was the advantage of the SPAS-12: one was just like another within the same model. He suddenly thought of something funny. With the Consortium helping to find the house and arrange the rental, had the house been insured? Lawsuits. Probably the owner of the house would sue him for negligence in letting a gang of heavily armed men blow it up like that. Track shook his head.

"There," Desiree whispered. "I packed the wound as best I could. It should stop the bleeding unless we have to make a run for it again."

"I've been thinking," Track told her as she cleaned the blood off her hands with a Wash 'n Dri she had taken from his pack. He was sitting up now. "When they come, I'll hold them off. You think you can make it through that back door yourself?"

"No. If I live with you, I live with you. If I die with you, then I do that, too. End of discussion."

"You're incorrigible."

"I'm not," she told him, smiling. She started unwrapping the sandwiches. He wasn't hungry, but he knew he had to eat. He took half of one and started to wolf it down. "Don't drink too much of this, but a little of the rum might do you some good." She was untwisting the cap of the metal hip flask.

Track nodded, taking a swig of the Myers's Dark Rum. It burned as it went down and the feeling was a good one. He passed her the flask.

He attacked the second half of the sandwich. There was still no sound from outside. If they had made the building, they could have LAW rockets trained on it and fire at any moment. "Look," Track told her through a mouthful of food. "If we don't get out of this I just want to say something. I never really figured I could feel for anybody like I do—"

Her arms closed around his neck and she buried her face against his chest.

She was getting him all full of sandwich crumbs, but he didn't care. "We'll make it," Desiree whispered. And then she sat up. She smiled at him. "We will make it, Dan."

Track nodded.

There was optimism and then there was blindness. He cursed himself again for the incident with the snowmobile.

It was his fault if she died. That it would be his fault if he died didn't bother him; he had always been responsible for himself. But that he would be responsible for Desiree's death... He lost interest in the rest of his sandwich and put it down, picking up the Scorpion. He had twenty-two rounds, total. Desiree had ten rounds, total.

He lied to himself, told himself that there was a chance. He started edging along the floor toward the corner of the long bar, the dust of decades streaking under the pressure of his body. Desiree was closing up the rest of the sandwiches and the flask of rum. She followed him.

As he reached the end of the bar, he could feel her opening and closing his pack. "Get the skis close to the end of the bar here, very quietly," he whispered.

Track could hear voices outside now, but couldn't make out the words. There were several voices.

There was no plan to formulate. He would have to play it by ear all the way.

Slowly, to avoid a betraying sound, he lowered the safety on the Scorpion. He braced the outside of his left forearm against the edge of the bar, his right elbow slightly bent.

Desiree whispered beside him. "I have the skis."

"Okay, stay behind me but cover my back in case they come through the back door on us."

"Yes."

"You're a good soldier, kid," Track whispered.

He waited.

The voices were getting louder.

And then the voice he had expected rose clear above the others. "Track, this is Hudson! We know you're in there. Make it easier on all of us. Kill the woman then kill yourself. It's the simplest way. I'll give you to the count of ten, then we blow the place to pieces. One!''

"LAW rockets," Desiree said emotionlessly.

Track smiled. "Someday I've got to thank that guy Hudson. Open up my wound again, get some blood on your hands, smear some of it on your right temple, then smear some of it on mine. Hurry!''

"What are you talking about?''

"Might be our only chance. Hell, it is our only chance!''

"Five!" Hudson's voice was louder now.

Track felt her fingers against his wound, and he closed his eyes against the pain. "Now, repack it quick. We're going to be moving. When I say run, just do it. I'll be right with you. If I'm not, I'm dead, so there won't be any sense waiting.''

Desiree nodded.

"Give me a kiss, kid," he told her.

She kissed him full on the lips. Track took her .38 and fired it once into the far interior of the bar. Then he fired it a second time. He kept his left hand behind the bar with the Scorpion in it, the safety downed. In his right hand was the Model 60. He stretched forward across the floor, the pistol near his head, his face turned to the side, the artifically bloodied right temple up. Desiree had done the same, but most of her body was behind the bar.

"Track?" The counting had stopped. It was Hudson's voice. "Track? If you're still alive in there, you'll wish you had killed yourself!''

Another voice. "Shit! They really did it.''

"Shut up, Greenwald. Kick in that door!''

Track heard the sounds of the door being smashed through.

He heard heavy running footsteps. He could feel Desiree's hand tightening against his left ankle.

He wanted to say something to reassure her, but to have moved or spoken would have meant instant death.

Track held his breath, waiting.

"I'll be damned! Killed the girl and then himself. Look!" the second voice exclaimed.

"Go check 'em. I'll cover you and McCormick."

There were no dramatic sounds of bolts being opened or slides being worked, all of that would have been done already. He heard footsteps, and he tried to remember the exact distance across the saloon floor.

The footsteps grew louder.

"Dead, I think."

"Think doesn't mean shit. Put a burst into him and then into the woman. Cold as a witch's tit in here," Hudson called.

Track rolled to his side, the Model 60 in his right hand, the Scorpion in his left, both pistols firing upward: the 60 into a tall, thin white man with glasses, a MAC-10 in his fists; the Scorpion into a huskily built black man with an M-16. The noise of the two pistols in the confined space was deafening. "Back!" Track shouted at the top of his lungs, pulling himself up and back, his leg telling him not to, the end of the bar disintegrating under a burst of assault rifle fire from Hudson at the door.

Track breathed.

He heard the sound of part of the door shattering.

He looked out. The white man and the black man were dead, and Hudson was gone through the open door. He could hear Hudson bellowing. "Get the rockets on the place! Greenwald and McCormick are dead!"

Track was up, his leg being washed with new blood. He stuffed the 60 into the right pocket of his parka, the Scorpion into the left. "Desiree—"

"I'm already getting them."

Their guns, their ammo. She tossed him the MAC-10. From the size of the hole at the muzzle it was a .45.

The M-16 was slung across her back. Then a pistol belt. He secured it around his waist. She draped the second pistol belt across her body like a bandolier. She tossed him a musettelike magazine carrier for the MAC, and Track pulled it across his shoulders and picked up the skis. Starting for the back door, he stumbled but caught himself.

He could see the doorway she had told him about. The boards looked less weathered than the ones outside.

He could hear something like a muffled explosion. "Look out!"

Desiree collapsed against him, both of them looking to the center of the saloon. Chunks of the roof were collapsing, a fireball belching skyward, the roar deafening.

Track shoved her away, swinging the MAC-10 on line with the back door. "Saw this in a movie once," he shouted and then fired, losing anything she might have said in the noise of the gunfire. There was a second explosion, and the floor started to cave in. But there was a silhouette cut in the boarded-over doorway, a silhouette carved in bullet holes. He threw his body weight against it, and the door collapsed. Track fell through into the snow, Desiree right behind him. The left ski went on. The right ski. Her skis were on and she helped him up.

Track let go of the MAC, letting it hang on its sling. There was another explosion, and the saloon was an inferno of rubble, the flames searingly hot.

Track dug in his poles, Desiree beside him. She was right about the hundred yards, but he could not see what lay beyond the drop-off. He slid ahead, digging in his poles harder. Desiree was outdistancing him. Twenty-five yards. Another explosion behind him. The rattle of subgun fire and then something heavier, an M-60 machine gun, he guessed.

Track kept moving. "Go for it. I'm right behind you!" Desiree pushed herself up and jumped, disappearing over the drop-off.

Track dug in his poles once more, tried bending his knees, but the left leg didn't want him to do it. Half stumbling on his skis, he was over a ridge of hard-packed snow that was the consistency of ice.

He looked back. The saloon was vaporized now. He could see figures of running men. He could hear the sounds of engines being fired—the snowmobiles.

Below him, the slope was steep. Moguls of enormous proportions were visible dotting the hillside, and from the top it appeared that wherever there wasn't a mogul there was a pine tree.

He was moving, bringing up one hand to pull down his toque, digging in his poles once and twisting in mid-air. He came down too hard on the wounded leg. He sagged forward into the snow. Desiree was several hundred yards ahead of him. Track felt tears coming into his eyes from the pain. "Dammit," he snarled. Blood stained the snow beside his leg.

He rolled onto his side, forcing himself up on his skis. If he could get up enough speed, he told himself, he could coast the left ski, keeping pressure off it.

He convinced himself that that would work, but doubted his own depth of conviction. The snowmobile engines were getting louder now. He let his poles dangle by their wrist straps and grabbed the MAC, working off the safety. A snowmobile rocketed over the crest of the slope. Track fired the MAC, emptying the stick into the undercarriage of the machine.

There was a terrific explosion, and a fireball of black and orange belched skyward. Debris rained down and marred the pristine whiteness of the snow.

Track let the empty subgun fall to his side, dug in his poles, twisted, then lowered his body as he dug in his poles again, starting down the slope after Desiree.

From the first moment he tried it, the coasting with his left ski wasn't working, his leg telling him to lay down and die. His mind told his body otherwise. Track dug in his poles again, then drew them up at his sides, narrowing his silhouette, bending over his skis like a downhiller, glancing back once. Another snowmobile was in pursuit. He bent farther forward, the wind tearing at him, the falling snow lashed by the wind against his body, the toque doing him little good, his face numbing with the cold and the wind.

He kept moving.

The angry sound of the snowmobile was growing louder.

Track ripped off his left glove and reached for the Scorpion .45 beneath the Velcro flap of the patch pocket. He stabbed the pistol behind him, twisting his head to see, wiping down the ambidextrous safety. He fired over and over, until the pistol was empty, the slide locked back.

He found the slide stop and let it down, then stuffed the empty pistol back into his pocket.

He kept moving, catching up his pole again, tucking it up.

From the sound of the snowmobile, he could tell the enemy was gaining.

And then he could see Desiree near a bracken of pine trees. The M-16 was up to her shoulder in a firing position. Track brought down his poles, dug in and twisted hard left, angling out of the path of the snowmobile. He heard the crack of the M-16, a 3-round burst, then another and another.

An explosion ripped the air. Track looked back; the snowmobile was lost in a ball of flame, rolling down the slope.

Track shouted to Desiree, ''Come on, hurry!''

He looked to his right. She was already moving, skiing parallel to him perhaps a hundred yards away. He guided himself right a little to intersect her course down the slope.

As the roar of the fireball died, he could hear the sounds of more snowmobiles.

He didn't look back; it would have been useless.

They were alive, at least for now.

His leg screamed pain again, and he told it to ''Fuck off!''

21

George Beegh stood beside the Sno-Cat. "It was over that way, I'm sure of it."

Baslovitch leaned out the open driver's door. "I heard it, too, but I couldn't tell the direction."

George turned around to look away from Baslovitch and in the direction from which he had heard the muffled sound of an explosion. "How far are we from Fat Woman's Creek?"

"Another twenty miles or so, in the same direction you are looking."

George started around the front of the vehicle, climbing aboard, saying nothing else as Baslovitch put the machine into gear. George picked up one of the items he had kept in the back of his Jeep. A SPAS-12, just like the one his uncle habitually used.

He had left the gun unloaded and cased. But now, tossing the case behind him, he started feeding the 8-round magazine tube, alternating slug loads and double O buck. He worked the magazine disconnect, fed a ninth round into the chamber, then let the bolt fly forward. He set both safeties.

"Anticipation?" Baslovitch murmured.

"Yeah," George muttered. He kept the SPAS-12 across his lap, holding on to the passenger grab handle mounted along the dashboard. The terrain had become steadily rougher as they had climbed throughout the late morning and early afternoon. It was hazardous moving at speed, because with the great amounts of snow that had fallen, sometimes it was impossible to tell where ground ended and air began. Twice they had stopped to dig themselves out rather than risk breaking one of the half-track's treads.

The cold had been numbing them and the snow fell incessantly. He had thought of his uncle then, and he thought of him now. Track was wounded. How badly, George did not attempt to guess. Perhaps Track was alone. Or if he was with Desiree, George knew his uncle well enough to realize that Track's primary concern would be her safety. And this Stone Hudson. How many men would Hudson have with him? George dismissed the idea of Hudson going against his uncle virtually alone. "Converge on Fat Woman's Creek," the intercepted radio message had said. Converge. The very word implied many men, perhaps vehicles.

George looked at Sergei Baslovitch and wondered if Baslovitch was driving them to their deaths, or to his uncle's funeral....

DAN TRACK LAY AT THE BASE of the slope, Desiree kneeling in the snow beside him. The leg wound was too bad now. He had fallen from his skis and rolled perhaps fifty yards through the snow before crashing to a stop. The entire trouser leg below the wound and for a space above it was saturated with blood.

"You're going on without me. It's the only chance for either of us. We don't know how many of them are behind us. I figure we've taken out eight of them. Maybe it's only Hudson and one other guy, who knows? But you leave me the rifle. There's plenty of ammo for it. You can bind up the leg and leave me the Thermos blanket. They'll be regrouping, then starting down the slope.

"I can't travel but you can. I can hold them off. Maybe stop them cold." He laughed. Everything was cold. He hadn't told Desiree, but he was feeling the wash of nausea that preceded passing out from loss of blood. He was fighting to stay conscious now, because if he passed out she would never leave him. "You can go and get help. There's a town maybe seventy miles from here, probably less than that. You can travel the rest of the day. It's mostly downhill. You should make it there sometime tomorrow night. Then come back with help. I'll be fine, as long as I don't move the leg, I'll be fine."

"No."

"Yes!" Track told her. "It's the only chance either of us has—the only chance I have. If we kill Hudson and his men, what's to say one of their snowmobiles will still be operational? How are you going to get me to a town like this?" And he gestured to his leg. "The faster you leave, the sooner you'll be back." He took her little revolver from his pocket and handed it to her. "Fill up the cylinder. I think there's one round left. Then get out that blanket and leave me another sandwich and get out of here. You're such a good cook, you've got me hooked on the things. I'm a turkey sandwich junkie."

"Dan—"

She was seeing the logic of it, he knew. He brushed snow away from his face. "Best case scenario is I get them all and one of the snowmobiles is still functional. I can take it and catch up with you." He laughed. "We can hit that town in style, huh?"

"Dan—"

"I won't die. Would I die on you? Don't be ridiculous! There isn't that much daylight left; take off fast."

"I can't leave you."

"Do it or we're both dead. I'll never make it out of here if you don't, kid."

Her eyes rimmed with tears, and with his bare right hand he brushed the tears away. "I can't!" she screamed at him.

"You've got to," he shouted. "Now go on, get out of here."

"Dan, don't make me leave you!"

"Get out of here—and do it now before they come again. Do it now!"

She leaned back from him. She shook her head and sagged forward against his chest and wept.

DESIREE HAD COVERED HIM with the blanket after rebinding his wound. She had left him a sandwich and offered him the flask of rum. He was barely able to stay conscious. She had kissed him once, long and hard on the mouth. All she had said was, "I'll be back, I swear it." Then she had clicked her boots into her bindings and taken off along the base of the slope toward where the ground dropped off to the east. He had watched her until her silhouette had disappeared. She had left him because she loved him. He didn't close his eyes; if he had, he would have passed out. Instead, he turned himself in the snow to face the top of the slope.

Hudson would be coming soon. Track checked the M-16: a round chambered, a 30-round magazine in place and fully loaded, two more 30-rounders beside him on the snow. The Scorpion was loaded with one of the 8-round extension magazines.

Each of the men he had killed in the saloon had carried a pistol as well, and Track had one of these. It was a Beretta 92SB, of the type recently adopted by the United States government for military issue. He had two spare magazines for the SB.

The pistol was beside him now in the snow. He waited, fighting to remain conscious, blinking his eyes, squeezing them tight. The nausea was overwhelming.

If he could hold them for at least an hour, Desiree would have a chance...if the snow kept falling and obscured her tracks.

He shouldered the M-16, waiting.

And now he saw movement halfway down the slope—a reflected flash of light. A scope? They weren't going to use the snowmobiles. They were going to come at him, possibly with an envelopment. Track looked right and left. He was exposed on both sides.

Adrenaline was pumping through him. He could feel it, driving back the nausea, the light-headedness. As long as the adrenaline kept coming, he would remain conscious. But when it stopped, he knew he would crash—pass out.

Track licked his lips, the ski toque was gone, used to pack his wound. The goggles were suspended around his neck. His hood was up, but his face was numbing with the cold. He wore only his thin silk inner gloves so that he could manipulate his weapons properly.

He saw movement again.

He counted five men moving toward him slowly, inexorably. The sixth man—he knew there would be a sixth man—would be Stone Hudson. Hudson would be waiting at the top of the slope, waiting and ready to come in for the kill.

Track waited. There was nothing else to do because once the first shot was fired the shooting would not stop until all of them were dead, or he was dead.

DESIREE GOTH HAD LIED to Dan Track, and the feeling it gave her inside made her very uncomfortable. She had agreed with him completely—he could not make it on foot. Going for help was his only chance. But she interpreted going for help differently than he did.

She had skied out of his sight, and then begun the tedious process of herringboning up the opposite side of the slope along the south face. It was rockier, less snow, more trees. It would have made poor downhilling, but actually helped her in the ascent. At the midpoint, she had been able to remove her skis and climb along the rocks, the skis strapped to her back.

The MAC-10 hung at her side. She had two loaded magazines left, one up the well. She also had the second of the two Beretta 92SBs taken from the dead men in the saloon.

As she moved, she reviewed her reasoning. If Hudson had not followed them immediately on the snowmobiles, he had decided against using the machines in an attack. He had decided instead to send in his men on foot, or the bulk of them, at least. To finish Dan Track.

The logical place for the snowmobiles would be the top of the slope, well enough back that stray gunfire could not damage them. There would be at least one man guarding them, perhaps Hudson himself. Commanders frequently stayed behind the lines to observe the battle at a discreet and safe distance.

Desiree Goth kept moving. There was no gunfire yet.

She was nearly to the top of the rise, her hands aching from the climb over the ice-slicked rocks. The tips of her fingers were numb from the cold. Dan Track would be angry, even if she was victorious, but she could live with his anger, as long as she could live with him.

She reached the summit and crept left to where some of the rocks seemed lower, unfastening the skis and the poles and setting them aside. She stripped off her gloves, keeping only the thin silk undergloves in place. She shifted the MAC-10 forward, working back the bolt as slowly and silently as she could.

She peered up, over the rocks, the MAC-10 ready in her hands.

Two snowmobiles.

One man.

From the photos Chesterton had come up with, she couldn't be certain if the man was Stone Hudson—but she was going to stake her life on the belief that he was.

He stood one hundred yards from her, and in profile she could tell nothing of his features. Field glasses hung from a strap around his neck, the field glasses coated white, white like the snow smock he wore and the snow pants, white like the snow around him. His M-16 was taped with white camouflage tape.

His men, she knew, would be closing in on Dan Track at the base of the slope.

She had never shot a man in the back before. She started over the rocks, but then thought better of it.

If she made a sound and he turned, his rifle would be better able to kill her at a hundred yards than her submachine gun could kill him.

She settled back and took the Beretta from its holster.

The chamber was loaded. Slowly, she worked off the safety. At a hundred yards, she had no idea if she could register a killing shot. But she could disable him. She was confident of that.

She raised the pistol carefully, grasping it in both hands, her fists curling tightly around the grip, her forearms resting on the rock across which she watched her quarry, her enemy.

She drew back the hammer, not trusting a double-action pull, drew in her breath, released part of it, held the rest.

The front sight was squared in the middle of the rear notch. She held a little high.

She aimed for the imaginary spot between his shoulder blades.

She slowly squeezed the trigger, taking up the slack until no slack was left. She drew the trigger back.

There was an ear-splitting crack in the cold air around her. A blossom of red in the small of her target's back. Absently, professionally, she wondered what kind of ammunition had been in the pistol. Nothing very good to shoot so low in a weapon so inherently accurate.

The man's hands flew up to his face, and then the arms snapped away from the body, the hands groping at the air. She fired again, holding substantially higher, near the neck. Another splotch of red, this time between the shoulder blades.

The body toppled forward. Desiree Goth was up, running toward the nearest of the snowmobiles.

She clambered aboard, found the key start and turned it, watching the gauges come alive. A glance to the back of the machine and she knew why the ones they had destroyed on the slope had blown so easily—five two-gallon gas cans were secured there. If they were all like that...she glanced around.

She heard gunfire from beyond the edge of the slope.

The other snowmobile was just like this one, loaded with gasoline. There would be one or two more of them parked on the other side of the gutted saloon, but there was no time to get them. She set the pistol—still cocked—on the seat beside her, testing the snowmobile's controls.

She worked the safety to drop the Beretta's hammer, then started the machine ahead, toward the streak of red blood in the snow, toward the lip of the rise, taking it slow to get the feel of the machine—there would be no time later.

She stopped it at the edge of the slope, then stood up, the Beretta in both hands again.

It was an easy shot. She worked off the safety and double-actioned the 9mm once, aiming for the center of the five gas cans in the snowmobile. She turned her face

away, bringing her hands to her ears as the roar of the
explosion slapped toward her.

She worked the Beretta's safety again, then dropped
the pistol into the holster, turning to the controls of the
snowmobile now. The engine was revving. She throttled out and the machine rocketed downward beneath
her, across the slope, toward the gunfire. Dan Track was
fighting for his life, she knew.

The wind tore at her, despite the protection of the
toque, the goggles and the hood of her parka.

She reached down for the subgun, turning the snowmobile into a gentle left, curving it above and across the
edge of the battlefield, aiming the MAC-10 by feel toward the five figures in snow smocks with M-16s and
subguns.

She fired.

DAN TRACK SQUEEZED OFF ANOTHER BURST from the
M-16, dropping one of the attackers finally, the man's
assault rifle firing skyward as the body skidded along
the snow-covered slope toward him.

Suddenly, the air was filled with the sound of an explosion, and he immediately knew its origin.

"Desiree," he whispered.

Track fired the M-16 again, another 3-round burst.
A miss. He fired again. This time it wasn't a miss, the
man's body tumbling across the snow. He saw a snowmobile along the far edge of the battlefield, and recognized Desiree from the color of her ski outfit. She was
firing a submachine gun.

Track fired the M-16 again. His adrenaline flow was
dropping. He fought it. He shouted at himself, "No!"

And then over the rise came an orange half-track.
Someone was hanging out on the passenger side, firing
a SPAS-12. Track knew the sound anywhere.

Track got to his feet and started forward to close with the remaining enemy. They were cutting south along the slope, the half-track in pursuit.

Track fired the M-16. He sagged forward into the snow when his leg screamed at him one more time and suddenly felt hot with fresh blood.

22

Stone Hudson ran, his hands bleeding from the rocks over which he had clawed his way, gunfire still echoing behind him.

The half-track—he hadn't counted on help arriving. And the woman! She had killed Blanchard, shot him in the back. Hudson fell into the snow, picked himself up, then ran on, skirting the still-smoldering saloon. The smell of burnt gasoline was heavy on the air from the destroyed snowmobile he had passed.

There were two snowmobiles parked in the front of the saloon, across the street from it. He kept running.

Radio, he thought. Get help. He kept running, falling again, his mouth filling with snow.

His rifle was gone—he didn't remember where. He drew a Beretta from his hip holster, shifting it to his left hand. He ripped open the front of his snow smock, then the parka underneath, grabbing for the second Beretta in the shoulder rig there.

With a pistol in each hand, he ran to the front of the gutted saloon. The two snowmobiles were in sight, and they were both equipped with radios. He could contact the Master at Idatana, get the Master to get that homosexual helicopter pilot up.

How would he tell the Master? He had lost thirteen men.

Hudson kept running, dropping to his knees beside the nearest of the machines. He straddled the seat, jamming the pistols into the pockets of his snow smock.

He started the machine accelerating. It wasn't good for the engine, but he didn't care.

Stone Hudson had to get away. The gunfire had stopped—they would be coming for him.

In his left hand, he took up the microphone for the radio, "Hudson to base, come in base. Hudson to base, come in base. Over."

THEY HAD LOST THE TRAIL after some twenty miles and had spent the past hour searching for some sign that would put them back on it. Chesterton's feet were numb inside his boots. But Zulu moved as though the cold didn't bother him at all.

Zulu had said nothing during the past hour spent looking: covering an area on foot, then getting back into their vehicle, going on for a mile or so, never getting warmer, getting out again to fine comb the snow for some sign.

The snow still fell heavily, obscuring even his own footprints as soon as he turned around to look for them. But a snowmobile was heavier—there should be some sign. Wind drifted snow across the snow already there, smoothing it. And so they searched nearer to the tree lines for some sign, where the force of the wind was reduced.

Nothing. Chesterton started back toward the half-track. If anyone found a sign, it would be Zulu, he knew.

And then Chesterton stopped. He had almost stepped into it, obliterated it. "Zulu! Here! I've found something! Here! Over here!" he shouted, his voice raw against the wind.

Zulu was running, bounding through the snowdrifts like some wild animal rather than a man.

Chesterton dropped to his knees in the snow, making a circle of his arms to protect the precious marking from the viciousness of the wind. "Hurry!"

And then suddenly Zulu was beside him, shaking his big head from side to side and smiling.

"Trouble is," Chesterton continued, "which way do the tracks lead?" For indeed, there was no way to tell which direction the snowmobile had been traveling, east or west.

Chesterton looked at Zulu. The big African's head had stopped shaking, and his smile had receded to a perplexed grin. As if in answer he just shrugged his shoulders and turned away.

23

"He's not dying, but he could."

"I'm the same blood type as my uncle," George told Baslovitch. "You're the one with the survival courses in Siberia—think of something!"

Desiree Goth cradled Dan Track's head in her lap. They had hauled him into the Sno-Cat where it was warm, and Baslovitch had stripped away part of Track's left trouser leg.

Dan Track's face was white. "If the temperature was higher, I wouldn't be as worried. But with his body temperature already lowering, he could die of shock or exposure," Baslovitch whispered.

"Do something!" Desiree Goth screamed.

George turned to her, putting his arms around her. "We'll think of something."

"One of them got away," Desiree said, her teeth chattering.

"We'll get him, later maybe. It's Dan I'm worried about," George told her.

"Wait just a minute," Baslovitch said. George turned to look at the Russian. "I don't know if this will work, but it might if we can improvise the suction. George, find some sort of container. Desiree, you said you had some liquor."

"Will rum do?"

"Fine. George, get the fuel line off that snowmobile. Clean it as best as you can in the snow. Desiree, we've got a Coleman stove packed in the back. You can get some water boiling. We can use the spirits to sterilize the fuel line and whatever we can contrive as needles, and then we give Dan a direct transfusion—I hope."

"Is this going to work?" George asked.

"I don't know—I'd be a liar if I said I did. But in theory it should."

George looked at his uncle. He didn't want him dead, in theory or otherwise.

THE MASTER OF D.E.A.T.H. set down the telephone receiver very calmly. He stared across the desk. He had been using the plant superintendent's office all day, and the room was grubby, depressing. He stared at the calendar on the wall—a picture of a little girl holding a kitten on her lap.

He studied the picture. The little girl was pretty. He didn't like cats at all.

The Master of D.E.A.T.H. stood up. He picked up the telephone receiver, pressing the com-line button for the plant manager who was using the outer office, having displaced his secretary. "Menninger, come in please." He didn't wait for a reply, setting down the receiver.

There was only one thing to do.

He turned to check the wall map behind the desk. The words *Fat Woman's Creek* were barely visible.

The nearest town was Storm City. If Track was as mortally wounded as Hudson had indicated in his panic-ridden radio message, then whoever had been on the scene to effect the rescue would take Track there.

Hudson had outlived his usefulness.

The door opened and the Master turned at the sound. "Yes, Mr. Nichts."

The Master smiled. "I have a job that needs doing. How many security personnel do we have stationed about the factory?"

"We have fifty-six men available, and they work in three shifts, as you know, sir."

"Leave one shift on. I want the other three dozen or so of them here within the hour. Have them called or whatever you do. I will meet with them. They should be dressed for cold weather, extreme cold. See to it that the armory is opened for them to supply whatever their needs might be."

"But sir—"

"I have no time for debate. Also, issue automatic rifles to each of the men now on duty and send me the security supervisor."

"He's at home, sir."

"Then get him, now!" The Master smiled.

He mentally dismissed the man and picked up the telephone receiver, pushing the button for an outside line. He worked the touch-tone buttons in the right combination for the house down the road from the factory.

On the sixth ring, the phone was answered.

"Herr Gurnheim, this is Harwood Nichts. I want to speak with Jilly Mason and yourself, down here. Immediately. Mr. Mason should be prepared to travel, and you should be prepared to do your ultimate work."

He hung up, not waiting for a reply.

The Master of D.E.A.T.H. turned to study the map. He placed his thumb over the name of the town where Major Daniel Hunter Track would soon be—and the Master rubbed it out in his imagination.

24

Zulu had taken the controls of the half-track snow tractor and Chesterton had gladly relinquished them. His arms ached from fighting the wheel over the progressively rugged terrain.

They had driven for more than an hour, and as he looked through the window of the tractor, he saw a splotch of something dark through the falling snow along the horizon line. "Zulu!" And Chesterton pointed to their right. "Turn, that way. Quickly!"

Chesterton felt the lurching sensation as Zulu shifted the vehicle's course. "A little back left," Chesterton cautioned, peering through the windshield, rubbing away some of the steam gathered there with the sleeve of his jacket. He saw it again—it was coming toward them. A snowmobile. They had taken the right direction after all.

"I see it!" Zulu's voice resonated like a bass drum. "I see it! Do not kill that man! Not yet."

Chesterton reached behind him and grabbed his Walther MPK subgun. He worked open the bolt. A man in a white snow smock was riding a black snowmobile. The man had changed the direction of his machine and was sitting across their line of travel laterally now, from left to right. Chesterton pushed open the storm window beside him, shoving the muzzle of the MPK through it, firing a 3-round burst high into the air.

The glass beside him spiderwebbed; the man had fired a pistol.

Zulu commanded, "You will take the wheel, Sir Abner, when I say. Then you will slow as we get alongside him. If he reaches the far slope, he can outdistance us easily. Be ready...now!"

Chesterton reached out, catching the wheel in his left fist, the Walther on safe and slung at his side. Zulu edged out of the driver's seat, and Chesterton awkwardly assumed Zulu's position behind the wheel.

The machine zigzagged sickeningly for a moment, and then Chesterton had it under control. "What are you doing?" Chesterton shouted.

"Bulldogging, Sir Abner. Pull alongside him. Hurry!"

Chesterton forced the machine to give everything it had as the snowmobile they pursued started to pick up speed as well. The ground began angling downward.

Chesterton felt the sudden cold rush of air as the passenger door was opened, and Zulu hung halfway out. The snowmobile swerved, the man at its controls firing a pistol again. The dome light in the half-track shattered.

Chesterton's teeth gritted. He cut the wheel hard right until he was nearly on top of the snowmobile. Zulu's Browning Hi-Power barked twice as the man in the snowmobile raised his pistol. The windshield of the snowmobile shattered, and the vehicle swerved wildly. The pistol in the man's right hand fell to the snow.

"Slow it now, Sir Abner!" Zulu commanded.

Chesterton eased up completely on the gas pressure as Zulu leaped from the door. The African was airborne for an instant as Chesterton watched, then Zulu's body swamped the man at the controls of the snowmobile.

Chesterton cut the wheel of the half-track hard left, picking up speed again to keep almost abreast of the snowmobile as the machine careered wildly along the slope. Zulu and the man behind the controls were fighting hand to hand. And suddenly the man in the white snow smock was airborne, pitched into the snow. Zulu jumped after him, both men rolling along the snow-covered ground. Chesterton began braking, bringing the half-track to a gradual stop. The snowmobile was moving on a vector toward a bracken of snow-laden pines perhaps a hundred yards farther along the slope.

Chesterton jumped from the driver's seat, running toward Zulu and the snowmobiler who grappled in the snow.

But Zulu was up then, hauling the man in the white snow smock to his feet by the scruff of his neck. Chesterton saw a flash of something almost black against the white of the snow—a pistol. Zulu's right hand lashed out, slapping the pistol away into the snow, then his hand crashed forward and down, and the body of the man in white visibly shuddered.

Zulu released his hold on the man's clothing and the body sagged into the snow at Zulu's feet, like a rag doll discarded by a bored child.

Chesterton slogged toward them through the snow, and as he watched, Zulu turned around, a strange smile on his face. "It is our much sought after Colonel Hudson. How fortunate for us. How unfortunate for him."

Chesterton stopped running.

The snowmobile had crashed into the pines.

Chesterton dropped to his knees in the snow and caught his breath.

IT HAD TAKEN TWENTY MINUTES before Hudson's eyelids had begun to flutter. Zulu had then slapped the man hard across the face and the eyelids seemed to almost spring open. In Zulu's right hand was the ornate Gerber knife. Chesterton had recovered two pistols from the snow, Beretta 92SBs, and Zulu had searched Hudson, recovering a third pistol—a 950B Jetfire .25, also Beretta produced—as well as two fighting knives. One was a boot knife, the second a survival knife the size of the Gerber Zulu now held in his right hand, poised against Hudson's protruding Adam's apple. "I shall ask my questions once, Colonel Hudson. Should I detect an untruth, you will regret the telling of it. Do I make myself clear?"

Chesterton was disappointed. He had expected more out of the career mercenary, assassin, madman by all accounts. But perhaps Hudson's obvious fright had something to do with Zulu's manner, his obvious sincerity, Chesterton thought, smiling. Hudson's jaw dropped and Chesterton half expected to see the snow turn yellow at the apex of the irregular vee Hudson's legs made in the snow.

Hudson almost moaned the word, "Yes."

"Where are Desiree and the major?" Zulu's hand moved almost imperceptibly with the knife, pressing its point slightly closer to the flesh.

"I don't know!"

Zulu backhanded the man with his bare left. "Liar!"

"I *don't* know. Last I saw them, the Goth woman was perfect. I mean, she wasn't wounded or anything. Track had a leg wound, losing a lot of blood. We were fighting and Desiree Goth got hold of one of our snowmobiles and a subgun—she counterattacked. And then an orange half-track comes down the slope. I couldn't see the driver. But that George Beegh guy's hanging out the side with some kind of shotgun. I got out of there—only one left," Hudson concluded dispiritedly.

Zulu leaned back in the snow, staring at his knife. He didn't look at Hudson. "Were you simply in flight, or had you a destination?"

Hudson didn't answer for a moment.

Zulu raised the knife. "Hudson, I would dearly love the slightest provocation that would justify my killing you. Or I could lock you in a room with George Beegh and let his considerable strength come into play. You see, your men in their attempt to kill George caused the permanent paralysis of the woman to whom George is engaged to be married. I should think George would literally dismember you...if I do not do it first. Choose your answers carefully."

"Nigger," Hudson sneered.

Chesterton started for the man.

Zulu rose to his full height in one fluid motion, holding Chesterton back. Zulu handed Chesterton his knife and his pistol. Then he started for Hudson, Hudson edging back along the snow—and now the snow did yellow between Hudson's legs. "Wait! Look, I'll tell you—"

"I'm afraid you are too late now!"

"Look, I was going to a rendezvous point. Jilly Mason was coming to pick me up. Take me to Idatana where the Master has this factory."

"What sort of factory?" Chesterton asked quickly.

"Some kind of poison gas and the gas turns into a germ or something and it still kills people. And then it degenerates again and it's harmless. He's got tons of the stuff there, gonna use it to blackmail the U.S. government—some kind of cockamamy scheme. Shit, man, leave me alone! Please!"

Hudson got shakily to his feet. Zulu slapped him down.

"What are the coordinates for the rendezvous?"

"They're on the map in the snowmobile."

"What time—"

"About an hour, before you knocked me out, anyway."

"Mason will be alone?"

"Yeah, he's supposed to be."

Zulu walked up to stand in front of Hudson. He wrenched Hudson to his feet. "Colonel Hudson. You will aid us, or I will kill you slowly and painfully."

Hudson only nodded his head.

Zulu threw the man down into the snow.

"My God," Chesterton whispered. "Mason! Poison gas!"

"Quite," Zulu said, prodding Hudson ahead of him toward the wrecked snowmobile.

25

They had not been able to move the vehicle while the transfusion was underway, and to avoid going mad, Desiree Goth had gone for a walk, taking with her the MAC-10 submachine gun. Despite the bitter cold, it was better than sitting inside with nothing to do but wait.

After a time, she tired of walking and took the snowmobile she had driven into the battle back up the slope toward the ghost town. They had not needed the snowmobile's fuel line for the transfusion, using instead a clean spare packed away for the half-track.

She stopped the snowmobile some fifty feet from the height of the slope, almost beside the body of the man she had shot in the back. Holding the MAC in an assault position, she moved closer to the body. She had to know if it was Stone Hudson she had killed, because she wanted the man dead. Badly.

She pushed the body with her boot. It was rigid.

The eyes behind the ski toque were open, but snow covered them.

She looked along the slope to be certain she was alone.

She pulled back the ski toque. The man had blond hair. Hudson didn't. The skin on the face was blue, and she drew the toque back down as best she could, recoiling from the visage.

Climbing aboard the snowmobile again, Desiree started the machine up the slope, the snowmobile skidding laterally a little just as it reached the top. She skirted the burned remains of the snowmobile she had destroyed and went around the gutted saloon.

In the street in front of the saloon was one remaining snowmobile. She knew now that Stone Hudson had gotten away. Dismounting, Desiree walked forward, the MAC still in an assault position. Perhaps a map had been left behind in the second snowmobile; there had been nothing of interest in the one she drove.

She stopped. In front of the spare gasoline cans at the back of the machine there was a blanket, the blanket obviously draped over something.

She shifted the MAC into her right hand and flipped back the olive-drab snow-covered blanket. She started to laugh. In front of her was a SPAS-12 shotgun, a Smith & Wesson Model 686 revolver and two Norwegian army engineer's bags.

All of it belonged to Dan Track. Desiree Goth closed her eyes.

TRACK OPENED HIS EYES. His mouth was very dry and his left arm ached with a strange pain, almost as if there were a…he looked to his arm and saw a needle, of sorts. The needle was connected to a piece of tubing that looked like a fuel line. He followed the tubing with his eyes. It ended at another improvised needle, stuck into another arm.

He followed the arm to the face. "George? What the hell are you doing here?"

George Beegh smiled. "Well, it's a long story."

Track suddenly felt cold, and he looked toward the source. He was in the back of a vehicle the size of a small, squat truck, and the passenger door had just opened.

"Desiree...."

She clambered quickly from the doorway, throwing herself to her knees beside him, kissing his face. "Dan, you're—"

"Told you they couldn't kill me, kid." And Track looked past her. "Sergei? With a beard?"

"I told ya," he heard George say without looking at him. "It's a long story." George started it and since Track felt too weak to do anything else he lay there and listened. He discovered George had been right, it was a long story indeed.

JILLY MASON GUIDED the Bell Jet Ranger III downward, the helicopter handling well despite the cold and the blowing snow. He had downgraded the weather conditions from a blizzard to a snowstorm. Conditions were vastly better than when he had flown across the Idaho border the first time and tested the Master's gas on the pickup truck.

He checked the controls for the delivery system. The lights on the panel indicated the system was functional. He didn't understand anything more about it than how to use it.

He could see a snowmobile in the distance and he altered course slightly to rendezvous with his target.

He could faintly discern the figure of a man seated in the snowmobile. He would have thought Colonel Hudson would have been waving or something, but Hudson, the one time Mason had met him, had been a dour kind of person. Very unfriendly.

He had met numerous men in his life who were not gay nor even ever so slightly inclined toward it. And sometimes he had fantasized about "converting" them to the pleasures he enjoyed. But Stone Hudson was not one of these. Decidedly straight—thoroughly unpleasant.

Mason thought about the boy. He wasn't going to let the Master kill the boy, despite the boy's uncooperativeness. The boy was too pretty to be killed.

He made a pass over the snowmobile and he could see Hudson moving, looking up, but still not waving.

"Bitch." Mason smiled. He turned the machine into the wind, crossing two hundred feet over the snowmobile, getting slightly past it before he hit the toggle switch to release the gas. The compressed gas billowed behind him as he looked back, a gray cloud, descending rapidly, engulfing the snowmobile and the man who sat aboard it.

"Goodbye," Mason said, bringing the chopper up fast, hovering at six hundred feet.

He checked his wristwatch intently, waiting until five minutes had passed. He hummed a pleasant song, and wondered what the Master expected of him. "Check the body to be absolutely certain, Mr. Mason." Probably the Master expected him to jump Hudson's bones even though the man was dead. The Master was a very odd man.

And crazy.

Mickey Mouse's little black arm with the hand on the end of it had moved five minutes. He decided to wait another five minutes, just to be sure. He didn't trust the Master at all. What if the Master wanted him dead, too?

Exactly twelve minutes had passed before he touched the machine down in the snow. The semirigid two-bladed rotors made an artificial blizzard around the helicopter as he climbed out. It was cold, but he pulled off his right glove and drew the .45 from under his light blue ski jacket. He had carried a .45 in Vietnam, but he didn't like it. The image was so horribly macho.

He walked toward the snowmobile. He could see Hudson's body slumped over the controls.

"Colonel!"

Hudson didn't move.

Mason shrugged again and kept walking, his gloved left hand working back the slide, leaving the hammer cocked, the safety down.

"Colonel Hudson!" Mason singsonged the name. "Dead, are we? What a pity—you whore!"

He stopped within six feet of the machine. It was perfectly safe to be that close, but not to touch.

He aimed the .45 and pulled the trigger. The body thudded with the impact. He pulled the trigger again. And again. The body rocked from the machine and rolled to the snow on the opposite side.

"Drop the pistol, Mr. Mason."

What a voice, Mason thought, turning toward it, ready to shoot. But a shotgun was aimed at his head, held in one monstrous black hand. The body that belonged to the shotgun was huge, beautifully huge. And the man and the shotgun were less than ten yards from him. "I can explain," Jilly Mason began.

He heard a second voice; he knew this voice. It was Sir Abner Chesterton, the Englishman.

"I daresay I'd love to hear your explanation, Mr. Mason. Really I would. But at the moment, I rather fancy utilizing your skills as a pilot. So please don't make either or both of us shoot you."

"What the—"

The black man spoke. "Are you familiar with arms, Mr. Mason?"

"Arms?"

"Firearms."

"No—"

The black man's voice seemed to hold genuine regret as he said, "What a pity. Suffice it to say, the Steyr-Mannlicher SSG is one of the finest rifles made, and one of the most accurate. I had this rather excellent rifle aimed at the good colonel's head. His hands were tied. What is that gas you utilized?"

"I don't know what the hell you call it."

Chesterton spoke. "It's the same substance in that string of bizarre deaths I had George investigating. The green funguslike material is already blotching Hudson's skin."

Mason looked to his left, toward Chesterton. "Don't touch him—you want to infect us all?"

"I have no intention of touching him, none whatsoever. Poor beggar."

"The gun, Mr. Mason," the black man said. "Either put it down into the snow in such a way that it does not discharge, or I shall cause your head to suddenly disintegrate."

The black man had a really nice smile. Mason shrugged and slowly set the .45 down. It was heavy, anyway.

26

The Master of D.E.A.T.H. spoke to the men in the factory lunchroom, their bodies bristling with weaponry, their eyes fixed upon him. Just as he wanted, thirty-seven men including the security chief and Klaus Gurnheim. "Gentlemen. Whether you realize it or not, and I doubt any of you do, you are about to enter into history. However slight the role you play, it is important. Soon, you will leave aboard helicopters for the town of Storm City, Idaho. Two men and a woman are there who must be destroyed. One man is Major Daniel Hunter Track. The second man is Mr. George Beegh. The woman is Desiree Goth. These three stand in my way, and hence, in your way. To properly destroy them, it will be necessary to destroy the entire town of Storm City. There are easier ways—" he'd thought of the gas, but was not quite ready to use it on a massive scale, not quite yet "—but this is the way that must be taken. Every man, woman, child, dog, cat—every living thing in the town is to be killed. After all life there is destroyed, you are to burn the town to the ground." He smiled. "Are there any questions?"

No one moved. No one raised a hand. He had picked his security personnel well, he knew.

"Very well. I will not trouble you with the reminder that I accept nothing less than total success. And each of you will receive a two-thousand-dollar bonus when the job is done. Cash, of course." He allowed himself to laugh. He walked across the small wooden stage at the front of the lunchroom and down the three steps to the tiled floor. "Mr. Hempstead," he called to the security chief. "Pick six men who are the very best of the thirty-seven who are going. From among these six, pick the man who is the most ruthless, the most efficient. This man will be my field commander. Offer him a ten-thousand-dollar cash bonus, an extra thousand for each of the other five who will be his assistants. Then join me in the plant manager's office." He looked among the faces—Klaus Gurnheim's face seemed to be etched with anticipation. "Herr Gurnheim, I need your excellent services, as well. Come, we shall talk en route to the office."

Gurnheim's face appeared etched with worry. The Master of D.E.A.T.H. was coming to dislike Gurnheim.

He walked into the corridor and up the narrow stairs leading toward his office.

Gurnheim merely nodded.

The Master began to talk. "It is clear to me that this site is at risk. Whether as a result of the fiasco under the leadership of Colonel Hudson—who by this very moment should be the late Colonel Hudson—or through some other means I cannot foresee. Because of that, I am moving up my timetable. Tell me—" he paused to look into Gurnheim's eyes "—did you really suspect I had something so terribly mundane in mind as destroying a few cities and blackmailing the United States government?"

"But—"

The Master smiled dismissively, then continued walking. "No, Herr Gurnheim. I am giving you a chance to create the greatest pyrotechnic display known to man and at once relieve many of the world's most serious problems. I have developed a new strain of my gas that turns into bacteria. And I have also developed an antidote for it. With this and your considerable talent I shall realize my dream: total domination of the economy of the planet, and hence total rule. I will be seen as a savior. I will be leaving sealed orders for Mr. Mason to follow after us, because his skills will doubtlessly be needed. The bulk of my new gas is already loaded aboard aircraft that will eventually bring it to its destination. With the blizzard moving toward the southeast, we will be airborne within the hour. Now, I wish you to see to the readiness of the explosives I asked you to plant about this building. Then I wish you to join me. I was most distressed at the failure of our previous operation, and this is your chance to redeem yourself. Your last chance."

They stopped at the base of the stairs. "Mightn't you care to get started?" the Master asked, smiling.

"Yes, mein Herr."

The Master watched after Klaus Gurnheim for a moment. The man was obviously frightened and right now that was good. The Master began to ascend the stairs. He would give the sealed orders for Jilly Mason to Hempstead who would meet Mason at the field when Mason flew in.

Then Hempstead, his security director for the plant, would return to the plant, and all of the loose ends would be seen to.

Pleased with himself, he continued to mount the stairs.

27

Zulu held the knife poised at the throat of Jilly Mason. "I would like to discuss your reluctance, Mr. Mason."

"You don't understand. He's crazy. The Master of D.E.A.T.H. is a superlooney."

"All the better reason to visit his factory. But before we get into that, you will fly us to—" Zulu consulted his map "—the town of Storm City, Idaho."

"Why, for God's sake?"

"Storm City," Chesterton supplied, "was on George Beegh's itinerary. If he was stranded by the blizzard, it is likely he would have made it there."

"I suggest," Zulu began, sheathing his ornate Gerber MkII, "that a zigzagging course might well be our best option. Plot a straight line from here to this place Colonel Hudson mentioned to us—"

"Fat Woman's Creek," Chesterton supplied.

Zulu nodded. "Precisely, then plot a second leg toward Storm City. Zigzag over this second leg while Sir Abner and I scan the ground beneath for an orange half-track of some sort. Once we spot the vehicle, you will land. If Major Track is in need of medical aid, you shall have the inner satisfaction of knowing you have assisted him."

"You're gonna kill me anyway," Mason volunteered.

"Back to prison for you, more likely, at least until your next trial," Chesterton said gravely.

"I'd rather be dead," Mason answered, his voice low. "But I'll fly you. I don't have anything better to do." Mason's voice rose and he laughed. "Buckle up now, fellas."

The rotor blades started to increase their revolutions, snow swirling upward and around them with blizzardlike intensity. The craft began to ascend.

THE MASTER OF D.E.A.T.H. huddled in his fur-lined parka, watching as the Bell 206L-30 helicopters became airborne. His armada was on its way to Storm City. He smiled, then turned to Klaus Gurnheim.

"Shall we go, Herr Gurnheim?"

"To the helicopter, sir?"

"No, down the street and then to the helicopter. One matter remains at my rented house," and the Master turned toward his Mercedes and climbed into the back seat, shutting the door, watching indifferently as Klaus Gurnheim scurried around the front of the vehicle and started in on the opposite side. The parking lot he had used as his landing field was now empty except for one machine. If Jilly Mason returned in time, Mason would fly it. If not, then his personal pilot. He called to the man now, who also doubled as his chauffeur. "Charles—to the house."

"Yes sir, Mr. Nichts," and the Mercedes started across the packed snow of the parking lot toward the gates that led to the street.

But a police car blocked the gate, and as they drew near the Master recognized the figure of the local police chief.

"Charles—be careful," the Master cautioned.

"Yes sir," and the Master heard the reassuring click of the bolt on Charles's submachine gun that he kept under a blanket on the front seat.

The Mercedes began to slow, the police chief waving his arms to them. "I will talk with the chief, Charles, but be ready."

The Mercedes stopped, and the Master stepped out onto the packed snow. "Chief Schmidt. An honor, sir." He smiled.

"Mr. Nichts, there's a problem. And I'm not making any accusations until I hear both sides."

"How egalitarian, Chief Schmidt. And what is the problem?"

The chief still stood beside his vehicle, the lower portion of his body concealed behind the door. "Concerns a boy named Jimmy Hall and that rented house of yours. The woman next door heard glass breaking and she thought she heard screams. So she called me."

"You should have contacted me," the Master said, his voice low.

"Well, I thought of that, Mr. Nichts, I really did. But then I thought about all those security people you have protecting that factory of yours. And I started wondering why. So I drove over and stood underneath the broken window and shouted up. This boy Jimmy, he shouted back that he was a prisoner and something about being chained to a bed. So I broke in. I had probable cause coming out my ears after talking more to that boy. He insists you set him up with some guy who was going to sodomize him, but the guy didn't do it. And Jimmy insists you threatened to kill him. He also said you like being called 'the Master.' Now, you aren't by any chance the same Master fella that black congressman's getting that investigation all steamed up over, are you? Got some organization behind you called D.E.A.T.H?"

The Master smiled. "As a matter of fact, I am. Your skills as a detective overwhelm me, sir."

The police chief's body didn't move, but his right arm did and in his right hand was a peculiar-looking single-barrel shotgun. "This is a Remington 870, Mr. Nichts. It's nothin' fancy like them submachine guns your guards carry, but it is loaded with 2 3/4-inch double O buck, and to get off the first shot, all I've got to do is pull the trigger. So don't try anything funny."

"I'll confess, I know nothing about firearms, really. But that one seems most impressive looking, most finely made. Am I to take it I am under arrest?"

"For kidnapping, for contributing to the delinquency of a minor...I got a good healthy list."

"I'm sure you have, but I'm afraid I don't have the time to hear it. Charles!"

The Master threw himself into the open rear doorway of the Mercedes. The shotgun discharged. He heard the rattle of submachine gun fire from the front seat. "It's all right, sir!" Charles called.

"My God," Gurnheim whispered.

"You a religious man?" The Master laughed, picking himself up off the floor of the car.

He looked out into the snow by the police chief's car. Schmidt's body was riddled with bullets. The Master looked to the door panel of the Mercedes. It was perforated with too many holes for him to bother counting. "A quite effective weapon Chief Schmidt had." He smacked his lips as he pulled the door closed, glass falling from the window. "Charles, I think we'll fly on now and forgo returning to the house."

"Yes sir."

"Be a good fellow and turn the car around?"

"Yes sir."

"Under arrest, indeed," the Master of D.E.A.T.H. said quietly.

28

He found the thought an amusing one. Discounting metaphysics, a person's entire life was spent inside a human body, but the average person knew virtually nothing of the body's workings. Track could not understand why, for example, the warmth, the infusion of some blood and an hour's worth of sleep had made him feel much better than he had felt. They had slept side by side—he and Desiree Goth—in the back of the Sno-Cat. She was still sleeping as Track pushed himself into a sitting position.

George and Sergei Baslovitch were seated in the front of the machine, Baslovitch driving. Track called out, "Hey, George."

His nephew was up in an instant, moving stoop shouldered along the length of the machine and toward him. "You all right?"

"Yeah, fine. Wouldn't want to run a race—my leg hurts like hell. And that spot where you had the transfusion needle doesn't feel too good, either."

"Yeah." George grinned, rubbing his arm. "I know the feeling. You hungry or anything? We put a lot of soup into you."

"I remember," Dan Track told him. "Look, thanks for finding us. For the transfusion. The whole shot. How's Ellen?"

"Doctors say there isn't any change. Getting stronger every day. Haven't talked to her for three days. No phone service around here."

"I know," Track said as he nodded. "How's your dad?"

"Fine. I called him in Washington before I set out on this little deal for Sir Abner. He told me to say hi if I saw you."

"Consider it said." Track grinned. "Where the hell are we going?"

"Storm City, Idaho—about another thirty miles or so. Since the snow stopped we've been making pretty decent time, for this thing, at least."

"What's Baslovitch doing with you?"

"Storm City's where they got set up in their new identities. And don't call him Sergei. He's a retired West German cop named Peter Kroehler. Tatiana's dyed her hair, kind of auburn colored—pretty. Anyway, she's Louise. We're all old friends."

"A retired cop?" Track laughed. "Any idea where Sir Abner and Zulu are?"

"They were looking for Hudson last I heard."

"Same here," Track said.

"Desiree checked. He wasn't among the bodies in Fat Woman's Creek. He got away."

"Wonderful. Hopefully Sir Abner and Zulu are still looking then. What were you doing out here?"

And George explained his assignment from Chesterton to find some link in the mysterious deaths involving the green funguslike substance, that he was narrowing the search for the origin to somewhere along the Idaho-Montana border. And George told him, as well, about the death of the boy Morgan Mistral and how Sergei Baslovitch had surmised that the fungus began life as some sort of gas.

Track asked what he felt was a logical question. "Do you think the Master's behind this?"

George didn't answer immediately. He offered a cigarette to Track, and Track took it and broke off the filter. George lit his own, then held the flame for his uncle. Finally, through a cloud of exhaled smoke, George said, "I think it's the Master. Yeah. And I think he's got some operation somewhere on the Idaho-Montana border where he's testing this stuff...maybe even making it there. I want to get the bastard."

"We may have trouble," Sergei Baslovitch shouted.

George wheeled around, and Track called to him, "Where's my gun?"

"Which one? Desiree found your L-Frame and your SPAS and the gear for them. I put your .45 Trapper with them."

"Give me the SPAS and get me to a window," Track snapped.

Desiree stirred beside him, then suddenly sat bolt upright. "What is it?"

"There could be trouble. A helicopter is landing straight ahead of us," Baslovitch called.

George was already in the front passenger seat, a SPAS in his hands.

"Give me a gun, somebody," Track shouted.

"Wait!" Baslovitch said. "There's a man hanging out of the helicopter. My God, it's Zulu!"

29

It had taken an hour of flying back and forth for the helicopter to get them and their equipment into Storm City. After the first run in, Jilly Mason had been turned over to two state troopers Track was introduced to as Ralph and Harry. Baslovitch had taken over the helicopter chores from then on. No attempt was made to recover the bodies of the men who had worked for Stone Hudson, nor the body of Hudson himself. When Zulu had told them Hudson was dead, George's face had gone white.

Storm City's one doctor had made it back from where he had been snowbound since the last blast of the blizzard. He gave Track a quick look over, then promptly went to inspect the eight-pound four-ounce baby boy the chief of police helped deliver during the blizzard.

Both of the town's full-time police officers were still snowbound in the higher elevations and Track, lying on a cot in the jail cell nearest the door, had met the police chief for less than sixty seconds when the man had come back to the station to run an electric razor over his face and change to a clean shirt.

The doctor returned just as Baslovitch finished the last flight in with weapons and gear picked up from Hudson's dead mercenaries. Track could hear the rotor blades. "Let's have a look at you."

Track looked at the doctor. "What?"

The doctor grinned. "Doctors are always supposed to say that. I wouldn't want you running any races, but that's really a rather superficial wound in your leg. It was all that skiing that caused the blood loss and simply drained you of energy. As best I can tell, you didn't get any worse for wear with that improvised transfusion—might have even saved your life. Can't tell. You should be up and around in a day or two and you'll need a cane for that leg for a week or so. Roll over, Major Track."

"You talked to Zulu?"

"The black man—kind of tall?"

"That's the one." Track nodded.

"Roll over, Major. I'm going to give you a couple of shots. A penicillin derivative—you're not allergic, are you—and a B-complex shot."

"Give it to me in the arm."

"Shoulder, actually," the doctor said. "Fine, right or left?"

"Left."

"Want a sedative? You could use some more rest."

"What? You got shots on special this week?" Track asked him.

"Watch it, shots can be easy or shots can be painful," and the doctor winked. Track started rolling up his sleeve.

HE LAY IN THE BED for another twenty minutes or so, unable to sleep. He studied the layout of the cell and the open area beyond. He sat up, edged himself along the bottom of the cot and then braced one arm against the wall. Putting all of his weight on his right leg, he tried to stand. He made it.

He could see George from the position where he stood and he called out to him, not raising his voice too loud, "Hey, George. Come here!"

George stood up and walked toward him. "What the hell are you doing standing up?"

"Getting ready to walk. If Hudson got a radio message through to send for Jilly Mason in his chopper—"

But Mason, in the next cell, finished it for him, "He'll have told the Master what happened and the Master will have guessed you'd be brought here. And when I don't come back—"

"He'll send people to this town," George almost whispered.

"You got it. Two things," Track began slowly. "Get Jilly out there to his chopper and put him on the radio to the Master, right away. Had a problem with a bad fuel line, took care of it. But he killed Hudson first and he's on his way in. He passed over the battlefield near Fat Woman's Creek and saw us out on the snow, used the rest of his gas and zapped us all. He's coming in."

"How do you know I had enough of the gas left, hmm, smarty?"

Track looked into the next cell. "Remember how well you and George got along that time he was going to rip your head off back in Chicago?"

"How could I forget?" Mason snarled.

"How about George goes into that cell and really does rip your head off?" Track grinned, seating himself again on the edge of the cot.

"All right, so there was enough gas—if I was careful the first time—and I was."

Track looked at Mason through the bars. "Jilly, I'll say that. You always come through in a pinch."

"What was the second thing?" George asked.

"What?"

"The second thing. You said there were two things."

"Right," and Track looked down at his left trouser leg. It was cut partially away below his thigh and was still stiff with his blood. "Get me a pair of pants, and remember, you're taller than I am." Dan Track didn't feel like getting into a gunfight half-naked.

30

Track was forcing himself to stand beside the charge desk. He was winning the battle against the light-headedness. Desiree Goth stood beside him, and to-gether they listened to the state trooper named Ralph. "According to the Sergeant Nelson I spoke with via ra-dio from Idatana, they got problems. There's a dead police chief, for one. About a half-dozen helicopters belonging to some guy named Nichts left a chemical factory on the outskirts of Idatana. The chief went there to confront Nichts over a boy they found who'd been kidnapped. He claimed Nichts liked to be called the Master. The helicopters could have been heading our way. When Sergeant Nelson and a group of citizens went to the factory to retrieve the body of the police chief, they were fired upon. Nelson did some checking around. Should be about eighteen or twenty men in the factory—all heavily armed."

Baslovitch interrupted. "When George and I had Mason use the radio in the helicopter, we got some man Mason identified as the Master's security chief for the factory. Hempstead, I think was the man's name. They had sealed orders for Mason left by the Master. They wouldn't open them to read them. Hempstead said the Master would be sending helicopters back to retrieve Hempstead and his men."

"Bullshit," George said through a cloud of cigarette smoke. "I had Jilly ask about the other choppers around the factory. This Hempstead guy said they'd left on a mission for the Master. According to Jilly, we could have upward of three dozen guys coming at us."

"What kind of weapons they have?" Track asked. "And are the machines equipped to use the gas?"

Baslovitch shook his head. "Jilly knows nothing about guns. He said machine guns and rifles. I assume he means submachine guns. And what kind of rifles, I don't know. But he said his machine was the only one equipped to release the gas."

"Then it will be a gunfight," Desiree murmured.

"We should evacuate everyone," Tatiana interrupted.

"Where can we take them?" Baslovitch asked her, smiling, lighting a cigarette. Track noted Baslovitch smoked Camels now. "And besides, with one helicopter, there wouldn't be time. Mason estimated their travel time and gave them an ETA here—" Baslovitch consulted his wristwatch "—in less than forty-five minutes."

"What the hell will we do?"

Track looked at the second state trooper, Harry. "Find the safest building in town and get everybody into it, then set up a perimeter and defend it. Can we get the National Guard in here?"

"In about two hours, maybe a little more."

"How about state police?" Track asked Harry.

"In any force—at least two hours. Half the state is still socked in with this blizzard."

"Then it looks like we do it ourselves," George interjected.

Track looked at Baslovitch, almost using his real name as he addressed him. "How much flying time left on that chopper?"

"About twenty minutes to a half hour, but I wouldn't want to be in it those last ten minutes. And there's no aviation fuel available locally. If we had the time, I could set up the machine to run on automotive fuel, but there isn't time."

"Scratch the chopper, then." Track nodded.

Zulu, sitting in the far corner beside Chesterton, spoke. "I have listened to all of this. It appears that Major Track has the only solution possible under the circumstances. A school or a church, perhaps, place all the local inhabitants there. Any who might be useful to a defense could be made a rear guard—"

Chesterton interrupted him. "I'll check with our friend Mr. Mason that these helicopters aren't armed. Be right back," and Chesterton disappeared toward the cells.

Track told Harry and Ralph, "I'd like the two of you to find the police chief and start organizing this thing. Get the chief to hook you up with any locals who are good with guns. We can turn some good deer hunters into snipers. Bird hunters we can keep as a last-ditch defensive squad for whatever building we select as the hardsite. And we'll raid that store you guys told me about—"

"Mistral's," George volunteered.

"Right, take all the useful weapons he might have and all the ammo. Make sure those bird hunters have plenty of shells for their shotguns. Even skeet loads—at close range they can really do a number."

"I'll get a couple of local people and take care of that," Desiree volunteered.

"Zulu, you help her."

"Of course, Major."

Chesterton returned from the cell block. "As far as Mason knows—and I think he's telling the truth—

the helicopters aren't gunships, have no integral armament.''

"Get Mason out of here. Handcuff him to something wherever we set up the hardsite. Just cause he's a rotten son of a bitch doesn't mean he should stay here and get killed. The jail's probably the first place they'll hit.'' Track looked at Tatiana. "Louise, get some of the other women in town organized. Get food, water, medical supplies and move it all to the hardsite.''

"There's a Presbyterian church at the end of town,'' Ralph suggested. "A brick building, not too many windows in the sanctuary, we could keep everybody in there. Form a perimeter in the trees near the parking lot and around it.''

"Okay, let's do it,'' Track said.

31

Ralph had contacted the Montana state police and put Track on with a man named Manchester. "That's right," Track said into the microphone. "One of the men who works with the Master is Klaus Gurnheim, the Nazi terrorist. He's a genius with explosives. It doesn't sound to me like the Master has any intention of getting his people that he left behind out of there. He's probably got that factory set to blow sometime soon, and according to Jilly Mason the Master's got tons of that gas there. Over."

"Then you're suggesting that we evacuate Idatana in the event that this factory is rigged with explosives. Correct? Over."

"That's correct, sir. Otherwise, you're going to have a lot of dead people. If you can get a SWAT or some special operations group from the National Guard into that factory, you might have a chance of stopping it. But I doubt it. Gurnheim's good, very good. Over."

"Major Track, I'll have to check with the governor's office. But I'm sure of his approval. What about your position? Over."

"If we get out of this alive and we're lucky, we can commandeer some of the choppers the Master's sending and get to Idatana to help if it isn't too late. Over."

"Good luck to you. Will I be able to keep you advised? Over."

"We're pulling the radio from Mason's helicopter and setting it up in the church. Transmission should be weak but listen for us and we'll listen for you. Track out."

"Again, good luck to you. Manchester out."

Track handed back the microphone to Ralph. "Neutralize this radio, but not permanently in case we need it again. I don't want the bad guys using it."

Track, using a cane George had expropriated from Mistral's, started toward the doors and the snow-covered street.

He wrenched open the door, ignoring the pain in his leg as best he could, stepping out carefully. Cars and pickup trucks were moving through the street in a steady stream toward the Presbyterian church at the end of the town. Chesterton was the traffic manager, and as soon as a vehicle arrived he parked it with the gas tank facing inward, forming part of a circle behind which the townsfolk would take cover in the first stage of the defense of the town. Once their position was no longer tenable, they would withdraw, then turn their gunfire on the vehicles igniting the tanks and turning the cars and trucks into a ring of fire, if necessary.

The pickup truck parked at the curb was brimming over with firearms, ammunition and other gear Desiree and Zulu had scrounged. Zulu crossed nimbly over the snowbank and skated down to help Track. "I will never allow you to forget this, Major, that when you were injured I had to help you as though you were aged and infirm."

"Eat it," Track said with a grin. "But thanks for helping, for everything."

Zulu said nothing, and Track felt himself lifted across the snowbank and down the other side. "I can manage from here," Track told him, starting to climb aboard the pickup. Zulu slid in behind the wheel, Desiree between them.

"We've found everything that will shoot and a few things that are doubtful. Harry tells me he has seventeen men with rifles with telescopic sights on the roof of the church. He has another ten with rifles with iron sights already around the wall of vehicles. Just inside the church he has eighteen shotgunners ready for the last-ditch defense if it gets that bad. I'm keeping the assault rifles and submachine guns we scrounged from Hudson's men for ourselves—there's a limited supply of 5.56mm and 9mm ammo for those."

Track nodded. "Good thinking." The truck was starting to move now, blending into the flow of traffic toward the church.

Desiree continued speaking. "Tatiana has all the food and water she could find, and milk for the children already inside. These should be the last of the vehicles to form the first perimeter. Ammunition could become a critical problem. We cleaned out Mistral's store and all of the citizens have brought their own ammunition, but we still don't have that much. I can get a precise count if you think it would be useful."

"Just an estimate," Track told her, lighting a cigar, his window cranked down all the way despite the cold.

"The rooftop snipers have an average of a hundred rounds each—just deer hunters. They weren't ready for a war. The trouble we have is that there must be eighteen or twenty different caliber rifles in use."

"Aww, wonderful," Track said, groaning. "I don't see this as something that's going to last for days. The food and water are just a precaution. We could have National Guard troops in here in another two hours according to the dope Ralph got off the radio a few minutes ago. It's a matter of surviving the first assault, and that should be a hard one."

"They will encounter more than they bargained for," Zulu observed.

"But as long as they're airborne, we'll be spraying lead like crazy at them—that's the problem," Track told him. "Just hope for the best."

Zulu was turning into the road that fronted the church's parking lot, Chesterton waving them ahead, the police chief aiding Chesterton with traffic management. Zulu parked the truck well back from the ring of vehicles. Some of the townspeople came up to it and started to unload the weapons and other gear under George's direction as Track climbed down. Track shouted to Zulu across the noise, "You get Ralph and Harry up on the roof with automatic weapons, Zulu. They can take charge up there and assault rifles might be the only defense against the choppers if they concentrate their fire on the rooftop."

"Yes, Major," and Zulu was sprinting off across the snow.

Tatiana ran up to Track, carrying his SPAS-12 and his two musette bags. "Here, I thought you might use these."

Track nodded at her as she went off toward the church. Track slung the musette bags across-body over his ski jacket, the SPAS in his right hand, the cane in his left. Desiree was beside him as he started across the parking lot and toward the ring of vehicles.

He glanced at Desiree. She was armed with a MAC-10 and two bags of magazines, the Beretta pistol in the flap holster of her waist.

Track caught sight of George conferring with Chesterton. Across George's back was a SPAS-12 like Track's. In George's right hand was a folding-stock military-model Mini-14 stainless, an Aimpoint MkIII sight mounted on the receiver.

Track kept moving, the cold not doing wonders for his leg, but soon he would be crouched on the blankets spread on the snow behind the trucks.

The last of the vehicles were pulling in, and Chesterton and the police chief were positioning them in the few remaining gaps in the ring to block all entry points to the parking lot. Women moved around the circle, older children with them, attaching rags to the gas-tank-side doors of each vehicle, the rags a precaution. In the event of an assault too quick to handle, the rags would be dipped down into the gas tanks then set aflame, turning each vehicle into a Molotov cocktail.

As the vehicles exploded, there would be a storm of shrapnel and glass. It would mean death for the defenders at the first line, but death for the attackers, as well.

Track reached the ring of vehicles. On both sides of him, men whose face he didn't know were taking to the improvised battlement, their firearms a bizarre collection of bolt actions and level actions, pump shotguns, handguns of every description: target pistols, silhouette guns, revolvers, automatics. To Track's far left he saw something that made him smile. A man in his fifties wearing fringed rawhide bags crisscrossed over his chest was deftly charging a muzzle-loading Hawken-style percussion rifle.

Desiree dropped to her knees beside Track and Track swung the SPAS forward, checking its condition of readiness. Satisfied, Track drew the L-Frame from the trouser band of his bib-style ski pants.

He heard the sound of a voice on a police bullhorn. He looked up toward the roof. Ralph had the horn to his mouth. "From up here I can see some dark shapes along the horizon to the east."

"That's them," Track shouted across the snow. "Be ready!"

Track got to his right knee, his left leg outstretched. He drew himself up to a standing position, bracing himself against the pickup truck behind which he'd taken over. Desiree was up beside him in an instant.

Track peered toward the east. The sun was lowering behind him, the clouds only intermittently covering the sky now, to the east the horizon darkening. But faintly now, he could make out darker shapes against it.

"Choppers," Track whispered. Then he shouted, "They're coming." And he remembered his father's words from so long ago, from those happy days when they had been together. "My dad used to tell me," Track shouted to all along the vehicular battlement, "that you don't shoot until you see the whites of their eyes. Which is fine unless they've been out drinking the previous night." There was some laughter. "Well, as long as they're airborne, we're going to have to shoot. Each of you knows the limitations of your own weapon or weapons. If a shot is out of range, don't take it. Save your ammo until they're on the ground. Once they're on the ground, let them get close until its a confident shot for you. And remember, you're shooting at men. I'm not going to give you that song and dance about these guys can shoot back. You all know that. But if the shot would be chancy on a deer, don't try it on these guys. Those subguns they'll have shouldn't be much of a serious threat beyond fifty yards. So leave the subgunners alone and concentrate on the guys with assault rifles. If they're good weapons and the men behind them are just fair, they'll be effective at well over a hundred yards."

And then he heard a voice from behind him and he turned around to see a man in a heavy overcoat and crushed fedora, glasses perched on the edge of his nose. "Since this is my church—your church, all of yours— let's bow our heads a moment and pray." The minister said nothing else. Track closed his eyes for a moment, feeling Desiree squeeze his hand. He raised his head, opened his eyes and watched as the minister picked up a white plastic box with a red cross on it—and first-aid kit—and took up a position at the battlement.

Track unclipped the sling for the SPAS, swung out the folding stock, then turned down the buttpale, re-securing the sling. He looked around the battlement. Zulu, George, Chesterton and Sergei had all taken up strategic positions behind the circle of trucks, cars, vans and Jeeps. A boy ran up to Track, an M-16 in his right hand, a grocery bag in his left arm. "The black man over there sent this to you, sir."

Track took the rifle, Desiree took the brown grocery bag. Track looked across the parking lot to the far side of the perimeter. Zulu gave him a casual salute.

Track looked at the boy—ten years old, perhaps. "Okay, now you get inside, son. I'm sure there's plenty that needs doing."

"Yes, sir," and the boy ran off. Track took the rifle and worked the bolt, chambering the top round—he knew better than to waste time checking the magazine. If Zulu sent it, it wouldn't be empty.

Track shouldered the rifle to get its feel, the SPAS on its sling at his side. The helicopters were closing now. Desiree, beside him, as if reading a shopping list, said, "From the distance they appear to be Bell 206L-30s. Good machines."

"I'm glad to hear that," Track murmured. He'd taken her to a movie once. A Clint Eastwood film with lots of shooting in it, and Desiree had mechanically droned into his ear each weapon's identification, each holster's maker.

The choppers were perhaps five hundred yards off, hovering now, holding back.

Whoever was their commander had spotted the defenses, was laying his plans. "Hold your fire!" Track shouted. "Remember, only when you know you can make the shot!"

His cigar had long since died in the left corner of his mouth and he chewed down hard on the butt of it now, waiting.

Desiree spoke beside him. "I'm glad you didn't say something stupid, like get inside with the rest of the women."

"I know better." Track smiled at her, waiting, watching the horizon.

"What do you think our chances are?"

"Poor," Track told her. "But we don't have any choice."

"Agreed, on both counts." She nodded. Her eyes were so pretty, he thought. His leg hurt like hell, but once the battle started he'd forget about his leg.

There was movement now. The helicopters were breaking off at tangents to one central machine, starting to form what he recognized to be a ring that would surround them from the sky. Then the attack would begin.

He waited, Desiree squeezing his hand tightly.

Soon all six of the helicopters were in position. He watched the one that had not moved. He didn't delude himself that the Master would be aboard it. Just an underling offered the chance of fame and glory, however fleeting.

The helicopter started to move.

Track shouldered the M-16, the selector set to Auto. He shouted, "Remember, let them get in range. Those aren't gunships. They have men aboard with assault rifles and submachine guns. You're stationary, shooting at a moving target. You'll have the advantage when it comes to accuracy!"

The noise of the rotors increased.

The wide passenger doors on both sides of the cars and trucks were open, and Desiree was shouting to him now. "The way the Long Ranger series is set up, two men on each side should be able to fire at once from the passenger seats. The men in the center seats will be able to serve as loaders. Only two blades on the main rotor and the tail rotor, so if any of our gunfire can bite into a rotor blade sufficiently, the ship could come down quickly."

"Too quickly, maybe, right on top of us," he told her, setting the sights of the M-16 toward one of the choppers streaking toward them. "Stay down. That squirt gun you've got won't do any good at this range, anyway. Spare mags for the M-16 in the grocery bag?"

"Yes."

"Good, hand them up when I—" He didn't finish the sentence as he fired toward the chopper's port side door as it started its pass. Gunfire strafed the surface of the parking lot, splotches of dark stains stitching across the grayed whiteness of the snow, lacing over the tire tracks, shattering windows in the rear of the church and in the vehicles that ringed the church. Track fired continuous 3-round bursts, the subguns opening up as well now as more of the helicopters made their passes. A body tumbled from one of the choppers as Track fired again and a man slammed into the roof of a van, crashing through it.

A pickup truck was on fire, flames licking from it, the gas tank hit. Track could see George wrenching open the pickup's door, jumping inside, firing the engine. "No!" Track screamed the wordceasing fire, unable to do anything else, watching as the truck rocketed forward, then back, jockeying out of the circle. "No...George!"

The truck swerved, peeling off a fender, ripping part of the bumper off the vehicle ahead of it in the circle, cutting across the snow-covered grass and toward the road. George jumped clear of the machine, rolling into the snow as the pickup exploded.

But George was up, waving as he ran, a cheer going up from the defenders now.

"Idiot kid!" Track shouted, laughing. Then Track swung his M-16 on line again as another of the choppers made a pass. Desiree's subgun opened up beside him. The chopper zoomed low over the parking lot, and the defenders in the circle of vehicles dropped under the trucks, gunfire hammered into Detroit metal.

Track emptied the magazine of the M-16, Desiree's subgun burning beside him. A dozen other weapons were firing toward the chopper from the rooftop of the church and from the parking lot. The helicopter seemed to hesitate for an instant, and then erupted in a fireball. The explosion was earsplitting at the close range. Track let the M-16 fall on its sling and took Desiree into his arms, shielding her head against his chest as fiery debris rained around them. And as the sound of the explosion died, a cheer went up among the defenders again.

Another chopper was closing, and as gunfire came steadily from the church roof, part of the machine's Plexiglas windshield shattered. The helicopter veered to starboard, then climbed.

"They're giving up!" someone shouted.

But Track knew better. He looked to the east. The solitary command chopper was starting to come down.

Track shouted over the din, "They'll be coming at us in a ground assault now! Can't afford to lose any more of their choppers!"

The other choppers were landing, as well, forming five points of a circle. Men were streaming from them, well out of range of anything but harassing fire.

"Hold your fire," Track shouted.

The volume of ammunition expended against the aerial attack had been enormous.

Track rammed a fresh magazine up the well of the M-16, dropping the empty into the snow. Desiree did the same with her MAC-10.

The men from the choppers had formed a ragged skirmish line and were advancing now, two-man fire-and-maneuver elements working slowly forward, running from cover to cover.

"Hold your fire!" Track shouted as a rifle discharged toward them from somewhere within the ring of vehicles.

The defenders had superior numbers. The attackers had superior firepower.

As Track stared out across the bed of the pickup truck, his blood chilled. LAW rockets. "Shit," Track snarled.

"What is...oh my God!" Desiree shanted.

Maneuver elements were working farther forward now, and Track could see that each man was carrying an assault rifle, a submachine gun and a pistol. From the distance, it looked like they had grenades clipped to their web gear.

The rocketeers were setting up, preparing to fire.

Track shouted to the defenders. "Go for the men with the rockets—those pea-green tubes that look like sections of sewer pipe. Anybody with a weapon that's good for long-range work—do it now!"

Track shouldered the M-16. The distance to the nearest of the men with the rockets was two hundred yards, but the M-16 was the best thing he had. Isolated shots started coming from the circle of defenders—bolt-action rifles, from the sound of the heavy reports. Track had moved his selector to semi. He squeezed off a shot, then another, then another, the almost negligible recoil of the .223 making his time back to target fast. Little spouts of new snow would spring up where bullets impacted, but none of the rocketeers were down. Track kept firing, more of the louder reports from some of the defender's bolt actions. One of the rockets fired, and Track watched its contrail as if in slow motion. It was coming for the center of the parking lot. Track pulled Desiree beneath the truck, his leg screaming with the pain. There was a trememdous roar and Track looked back. The pickup he had been driven in by Zulu was a giant fireball.

Another rocket streaked toward them and exploded. Track looked to his left. Part of the ring of vehicles was burning, a fireball rising skyward, black and orange. The smell of gasoline fumes was heavy on the air.

Track dumped the partially spent magazine, taking a fresh one from the bag. Men ran across the parking lot, their clothes and bodies aflame. Others were tackling them, hauling them down to the new snow, rolling the bodies or smothering the flames with coats and bare hands.

Track took his cane. "Take charge of this thing until I get back." He didn't wait for Desiree to reply as he crawled forward, pushed himself up to his feet. Once he was on the outside of the ring of trucks he shouted, "Every fourth man—follow me!"

As he started forward, he saw Desiree starting to scream, but Track lost the scream, lost all sound in the roar and then the explosion of another rocket.

He looked back once. Men were climbing over cars and out from beneath pickup trucks, bolt-action rifles, lever-action Winchesters, pump shotguns clutched in their fists, following him in a ragged line.

"Forward," Track shouted, throwing down the cane, lurching into a run, his leg aching like a bad wisdom tooth. The assault rifle was in his fists, firing, two spare mags stuffed in the pockets of his ski pants. Suddenly someone was beside him. George. "What the hell you doing here?" Track shouted.

"The same stupid thing you're doing, Dan!"

George was at his left side now, an M-16 in his hand. Track swung his left arm across George's shoulders, the two of them running side by side now, George supporting him as they charged toward the attackers. "Open fire!" Track shouted as he started pumping the M-16's trigger sending 3-round bursts toward the nearest of the attackers. Bodies started to twitch and fall, but more importantly the men with the rockets started to fall back.

There was a short burst from George's M-16 and then Track felt his nephew's right arm moving. "Hang on a second!" George shouted. The M-16 was hanging at George's side now, and the Ruger was in George's left hand. The Mini-14 started spitting fire.

Track buttoned out the magazine for his M-16. He gave up on trying to put in a new stick—if he moved his arm from George's shoulder, he knew he would fall. His leg was stiffening now and the pain was growing worse.

He swung the SPAS-12 forward, working off both safeties, tensioning it against its sling.

Some of the attackers were coming for them in a rush. Track fired, the SPAS churning a pattern of double O buck into the chest of one man, then firing again, this time obliterating a face.

The rockets fired again, and Track saw explosions to either side as he and George fought their way forward.

The pointmen of the attacking force had fallen back, and from behind positions of concealment and cover were returning fire.

Track shouted over the noise, "Withdraw! Withdraw! Cover yourselves."

He looked right and left. Wounded men were helping one another, starting back toward the circle of trucks and cars. Track fired the SPAS, turning with George now, George still firing the stainless folding-stock rifle. Track let go of the SPAS, letting it drop on its sling, and drew the L-Frame from the waistband of his ski pants. He stabbed the revolver behind him, firing it double-action. The subgunners were moving from their positions, advancing now.

Men on either side of Track and George were going down. But at the ring of vehicles, men stood on the roofs of cars, in the beds of pickup trucks, rifles blazing toward the attackers to cover the withdrawal. Track could see Desiree, standing atop the roof of a pickup, a lever-action rifle in her hands, firing.

There were twenty yards to go, and the attackers behind them were running forward with their subguns and assault rifles blazing. The volume of gunfire was maddening.

Ten yards. Track ran as best he could beside George. He stuffed the empty L-Frame back behind the bib front of his ski pants and drew the Scorpion from his shoulder rig. He thumbed down the safety and started firing. A man with a subgun went down, clutching his chest.

Five yards. George was almost dragging him forward now, and Track finally squeezed between a van and a pickup truck.

Ralph was at the improvised battlement, the police bullhorn in one fist, his revolver in the other. "Give me that," Track shouted. He snatched the bullhorn from Ralph's hand and squeezed the trigger in the handle. "Withdraw! Get away from the trucks! We're blowing them up!"

Desiree was at his side now, and Track put his arm around her shoulders as George and Desiree helped him across the parking lot. The rubble of the pickup truck that had been hit by the rocket was still smoldering and tongues of flame licked up from the downed helicopter. On both sides of them, men were running from the vehiculor battlement that would soon be a ring of fire.

The rear doors of the church stood open, and men crouched on either side fired past them toward the attackers. Track looked back once. The attackers were coming, starting to mount the vehicles from all sides, climbing over them.

Track shook himself free of George and Desiree, stuffing the Scorpion into his pocket, turning to face the attackers.

"Let's start shooting!" He rammed a fresh magazine into the M-16 at his side, then just held the assault rifle at waist level, firing on full auto, George on his right firing the Ruger, Desiree on his left, her subgun opening up.

A truck exploded, then another and another. Gunfire rained down from the roof behind them, and more of the trucks caught fire. Balls of flame belched upward, chunks of fenders and bumpers, shards of glass, trunk lids and hoods exploded skyward. The attackers were caught in an inferno of shrapnel and glass and flames.

The M-16 was empty, and he slammed the last 30-round stick up the well and started forward, George and Desiree flanking him.

The attackers, their bodies burning, subguns firing wildly, staggered around the parking lot. Defenders stood still, awestruck at the horror.

Track, Desiree, George, Zulu, Baslovitch and Chesterton—they were doing the work that needed doing, the killing.

32

There had been too many critically injured among the defenders at the battleground surrounding the church to do it any other way. Baslovitch had stayed behind to fly some of them to the nearest hospital. And Jilly Mason had been pressed into service, as well. Ralph riveted beside him with his pistol.

Track flew. He flew the helicopter despite the warning from the doctor that his leg wound had started bleeding again, despite the injunction that more activity would result in still more bleeding.

He flew. Desiree was with him. Zulu was with him. Chesterton. George.

Track glanced at his Rolex Sea-Dweller. In five minutes or less he should spot the Master's factory on the edge of Idatana, Montana.

There was nothing to say. They flew in silence.

Throughout the flight, he had been in constant radio contact with the Montana state police official he had spoken with earlier via police radio—Manchester.

Idatana had been evacuated. State police and citizen volunteers ringed the town; Track could see the human boundary now as he overflew it.

One more time he would try to defuse one of Klaus Gurnheim's bombs. But his luck was running out in that department and he knew it.

And still at least eighteen of the Master's security people were holed up inside the factory, ready to defend it.

Manchester had volunteered the services of some of his men—Track had refused.

Below him now the streets of Idatana were deserted.

Ahead, he could see the lights of the factory complex, a huge building at the center, smaller buildings at each of the four corners. It was lit as though decorated for Christmas and yellow lights washed the parking lot.

Manchester had asked if Track wanted power cut to the factory, but Track hadn't wanted to risk the possibility that Gurnheim had wired his explosives into the electrical system. Better to leave everything just as it was.

Track banked the chopper to starboard, beginning a lazy circle of the factory below them.

"I believe it would be wise were you to stay with the machine until we have located the bomb," Zulu said suddenly.

"Here! Here! Sterling idea," Chesterton added.

Track felt himself smile. He didn't look at them as he answered. "Thanks guys—you're just worried that if I get killed there won't be anybody to fly us out in the damn helicopter. The leg'll work as much as I need it to."

"Zulu and Sir Abner are right," Desiree chimed in. "I'll stay with you. You'd like me out of danger."

"I'd like you out of danger, but I'm not staying with the chopper. No dice," and Track let the machine hover over the roof of the factory, seeing movement below him.

"Three men as best I can tell from here," Chesterton called out.

"Four," Zulu corrected. "Someone pass me that bolt-action rifle." Track glanced back, Zulu wrenching open the portside door. "Shall I, Major?"

"Why not?" Track said. "I'll try to hold her steady."

"I'd suggest," Zulu shouted, the rotor noise loud now with the door open, "that it might be prudent for all concerned to cover their ears."

Track slipped his headphones back into position, hearing the hollow seashell sound for a moment, then the ground chatter from the state police and the local police. But even with the earphones in place, he could hear the muffled boom of the rifle. One of the men on the snow-covered rooftop almost seemed to fly for an instant, his body spread-eagling down. The rifle boomed again, and a second man sprinting for a doorway Track presumed led down into the building clutched at his back, falling in a heap.

Another boom of the rifle—it was a .375 H&K Magnum, suitable for most African big game, let alone men. A third man's body vaulted over the roofline and fell from sight toward the shadows.

There was no more gunfire and Track could not see the fourth man. He felt a tapping at his earphones and drew them down. It was Desiree. "Zulu says he can't get a clear shot at the fourth man."

Track looked back and grinned. "I'll land us on the roof, then you can get a clear shot at him. Hang on." Track sent the machine down. Through the starboard chin bubble just ahead of his feet he could see the rooftop clearly. The fourth man was nowhere in sight.

As the helicopter touched down, snow pelted upward and became caught in the downdraft and blew back toward them.

The machine stalled, and Track killed the engine and took the key.

He unbuckled his seat belt, then climbed out of the pilot's seat. He was horribly visible if the fourth man decided to shoot.

As Track started out of the machine, Zulu, Chesterton and George were already on the roof, their weapons at the ready. Desiree followed as Track stepped out. He had expropriated George's SPAS-12, and so had two of the 12-gauge shotguns, one suspended from either side as he settled the slings cross-body. Their stocks folded, he tensioned the one in his right hand outward against its sling.

If the fourth man poked his head up, he would die because all portions of the roof were covered.

Track shouted out in the still swirling snow, the rotor blades spinning lazily overhead. "Whoever you are—listen and maybe you'll make it out of here. Been wondering why the town was evacuated? Been wondering why the cops haven't stormed the place? Why the Master cut out—you know, Mr. Nichts? That's his name, right? Been wondering why nobody's come to fly you guys out with the rest of that gas the Master's been making here?"

In reply, an assault rifle was thrown from behind the cover of the doorway. Then a voice called out, "Wait a minute, I'm givin' up. Hold your fire."

Zulu shouted, "Come out with your hands raised above your head, empty and in plain view."

Track turned to Desiree, nodding his head toward the man who had just surrendered. "Smart people are so nice to deal with."

Zulu had advanced on the man, suddenly grabbing him, throttling him to his knees. Chesterton searched him; George and Desiree kept the rest of the roof covered.

Slowly, because his leg ached, and was stiff and bandaged very heavily against further bleeding, Track started toward the man, letting the SPAS in his right hand hang down at his side. "We don't have much time," Dan Track told the man as Zulu let him rise from his knees. "Klaus Gurnheim's a demolitions expert. We have every reason to believe he set this place to blow. I don't know when or how. But when it does, that poison gas you guys have been making will blow with it. If the explosion doesn't get you, the other stuff will. And from everything I hear, that's worse. Answer a few questions and you've got a ticket out of here," and Track jerked his left thumb over his shoulder toward the helicopter.

"All right," the man nodded fervently.

Track took a cigar from his black leather case and guillotined it, then lit it. It was his last cigar, the rest of his supply burned up in the rented house near Twisted Oak that morning.

Dan Track was very tired. It had been a day like no other.

"How many men are in the factory complex?"

"They're all in the main building—at least they were. Fourteen guys down there. And then—"

"And then what?"

"They kept the assistant to Mr. Barnes."

"Who the hell is Mr. Barnes?"

"Barnes is in charge of making the gas," the man said, his voice tight and nervous.

"What's the assistant's name?"

"Miss Duquesne. I guess it's Dr. Duquesne. I think her first name is Helen."

"Nice name," Track nodded. "What's she here for?"

"The gas has to be monitored, otherwise it will start turning into the bacterial agent—something to do with temperature. That's why they made the improved strain they had flown outa here."

"Improved strain," Track repeated. "There were orders left for Jilly Mason. Who's got them?"

"Mr. Hempstead. He's in charge of security here."

"What kind of weapons your guys got down there?"

"M-16's and Uzis, and each guy's got his own pistol."

Track nodded. "Where would Hempstead be?"

"Probably in the super's office. You can see the whole plant floor from the balcony outside. He has Miss Duquesne with him."

"You're a very cooperative man. If we get out of here, you'll get out of here," Track promised, meaning it. "What's your name?"

"Hal—Hal Chisnewski."

"Thanks Hal," Track nodded, then looked at Zulu. "Cold cock him."

Zulu's right fist laced across the man's jaw and Chesterton caught Hal Chisnewski, easing him down to the snow-covered roof. "Let's don't forget Hal, there," Track cautioned. Track looked to George. "Since they haven't charged the roof already, it means they're sitting tight and waiting for us to come down. George, you and Zulu take the fire escape—take it slow and careful on the way down—they might spot you through a window. Get to the ground level, find a way in and head for the superintendent's office. We need this Dr. Duquesne and Jilly Mason's orders." He looked at Desiree Goth. "You stay on the roof with our little friend. Cover Zulu and George while they make it down the fire escape, then keep anyone from messing with the chopper and watch our backs. Sir Abner and I are taking the inside stairs down.''

"You're just doing this to keep me out of harm's way.''

"No, but that's part of it,'' Track said honestly.

"All right,'' she answered softly.

Track nodded, then smiled at her. "Sir Abner, let's go.''

Track started for the doorway and the stairs that led down into the building. Behind him, he heard Desiree saying, "All of you—be careful.''

It sounded like a good idea.

He reached the doorway, skirting the dead man there, looking over the body casually. Chesterton picked up the man's Uzi. "Never hurts to have a spare,'' and he slung it on the opposite side of his body from the Walther MPK.

Track wrenched at the doorknob and drew the door back. No gunfire came at him from the lighted stairwell.

He worked off the safeties on the SPAS-12s, then settled both pistol grips in his hands. "I'll go first. They don't call these things alley sweepers for nothing.'' He started down slowly, because of his leg and because he had no idea what lay at the bottom of the stairs.

"Right behind you,'' he heard Chesterton murmur.

They weren't back lit—at least that was something on the positive side, Track told himself.

He kept moving, his left leg so stiff with pain he could not bend it.

Each SPAS was tensioned out against its sling, ready.

There was a landing and Track stopped there, Chesterton a step above, whispering, "Are you going to make it, Dan?''

"Got to.'' Track grinned, looking at his friend for a moment.

Track started down the next flight of stairs. Chesterton close behind him—there was a doorway at the bottom. "Should be waiting for us," Chesterton murmured.

"If they wait that long!" Track shouted, the door thrown open, Track pushing himself tight against the wall, firing both SPAS shotguns into the opening. His ears rang with the sounds as he worked the triggers in almost perfect synchronization, his body rocking, feeling the recoil in the fillings in his teeth. He could see Sir Abner crouched on the stairs, his subgun spitting flame.

The door slammed shut.

Almost.

A head was jammed in the doorway, part of it at least, the rest of the head and a mangled body sprawled at the base of the stairs. Another dead man had slumped in the corner near the doorjamb. "I think we got two more," Chesterton shouted, Track nodded. His ears still rang.

Keeping his position, Track began feeding buckshot into the magazine tubes of the Franchi shotguns from the musette bag at his side. Both weapons loaded, he started slowly down the stairs again. Behind him he heard Sir Abner change sticks in the MPK.

At the base of the stairs, Track stopped, working the numbers. Fourteen to start with according to old co-operative Hal on the roof. Two dead here, maybe two more beyond the door. That left ten at least, ten to be persuaded or killed.

Track edged toward the door with both SPAS-12s ready.

He nodded and Chesterton pulled on the handle, throwing open the door leading into the lighted main floor of the factory beyond.

Gunfire greeted them, and, Track flattened himself against the wall. He fired through the doorway.

Chesterton's subgun roared.

Track looked immediately beyond the door. Two more men dead, only ten did remain.

The shooting stopped and Track ceased fire, as did Chesterton. As Track fed more rounds into the magazine tubes of his weapons, he called out at the top of his voice, "This whole factory has been set with explosives by Klaus Gurnheim. You're all dead men unless I can figure out a way to defuse the devices. Give it up!"

"Liar!" The anonymous voice sounded somewhat lacking in conviction.

"I'm telling the truth," Track shouted. "Give it up. If this gas blows, a lot of people besides yourselves could be killed. You want to go to your deaths responsible for that? The Master's making chumps out of all of you! Give it up. We don't want you, we want to neutralize the explosives!"

Track waited. He always hoped logic would prevail but it rarely did.

There was a woman's scream—Helen Duquesne, he reasoned. Then the sound of a hand striking flesh. "Come and get us!"

Track chewed down on his cigar. "Hempstead—that you?"

"What of it?"

"Give it up. You know I'm telling the truth. Use your head, man, for God's sake!"

The only answer was subgun fire and Track tucked back as bullets ripped into the doorframe beside his head. Chesterton looked at him. Track nodded—open fire. The Walther started up again, as did the shotguns in Track's hands. The roar of gunfire was deafening, but Track heard the sound of glass shattering, the woman screaming. The doorway shredded under the impact of the metal-jacketed subgun rounds pouring toward him and Chesterton.

But then there was a new pattern: the sound of assault rifles from farther back along the main floor of the factory.

Track started feeding fresh rounds into each SPAS. Chesterton rammed a fresh magazine up the well of the MPK.

"Zulu and George?"

Track nodded. "Let's go," and Track started forward, firing both shotguns, Chesterton beside him, a subgun firing from each hand.

Men were running now. All of them wore dark blue coveralls and held subguns in their hands. Track could see Zulu and George in pursuit of the greatest number of them.

At the end of the factory floor there was one man, dragging a woman with him, the woman's body in front of him like a shield.

Track started along the corridor that ran between the vats and the machinery on both sides of him, Chesterton at his flank. Track shouted, "Hempstead!"

"Come any closer and I'll kill the girl, asshole!"

Track let both SPASs fall to his sides, the triggerguard safeties set. He nodded to Sir Abner Chesterton and Chesterton stopped. Track started ahead, slowly, because of his leg.

"I mean it—I'll kill her!"

Track shrugged his shoulders as best as he could under the combined weight of the shotguns. "Hey, look. If this was some defenseless girl you were using as a shield, I could see it, you know? But who is she— Helen Duquesne?"

At the distance, Track could see the girl's eyes flicker.

Hempstead shouted, "Back off!"

Track chewed down on his cigar. "Now, as far as I understand it," Track began again, "this young lady is the assistant to Dr. Barnes, right? Which means she helps Barnes make the nerve gas and the bacterial agent. And that means she's partially responsible for quite a few deaths already and was perfectly willing to be responsible for a lot more. You probably figured I'd like to talk to her, but if the only way to turn you off is to shoot a hole right through her, well—" Track smiled his biggest smile and raised his palms upward "—what can I say?" Hempstead didn't move. "So," Track told the man, "you put the safety up and then nice and easy set that thumb buster down on the floor, okay? Otherwise," and Track's voice dropped, "you're dead. I wasn't jiving about the explosives. They could go up any minute. The only medal you're going to get from the Master is a posthumous one for stupidity. Your move."

He didn't touch his weapons—there wasn't any need to. As soon as Hempstead raised his weapon, the girl would start squirming. It would make a first shot difficult. There'd be plenty of time.

"I want out of here," Hempstead snapped.

"I want the girl so we can have a little talk, and I want the sealed instructions left for Jilly Mason. Then you can fly out of here with us."

There was more gunfire from behind him as George and Zulu fought it out with the rest of the security force. There were still the explosives to find. He'd wasted enough time. "What's it going to be?"

Hempstead pushed the girl away and dived left. Track threw himself right as the .45 discharged. He heard the pinging sound of a bullet ricocheting off metal. Track's left leg buckled under him and he hit the floor hard.

There was no time for the shotguns, and he grabbed the L-Frame in his trouser band instead, double-actioning it twice into Hempstead's torso. Hempstead's body snapped back against a vat of some kind, then sagged to the floor, the .45 falling from limp fingers.

Helen Duquesne was running along the length of the factory floor toward the staircase.

Track swung the muzzle on line with her back and shouted, "Hold it, sweetheart—I shoot women, too!"

She froze and Chesterton ran toward her, his subgun in an assualt position. "Dan, are you all right?" he called back. "I couldn't fire without risking hitting you."

"I'm all right," Track said, getting to his feet, sagging against one of the vats.

He started walking as best he could, toward the woman, her dark hair making her pale face look even more pale. "Okay," he told her. "I want Jilly Mason's instructions. And I want to find out where Klaus Gurnheim put his explosives."

"I—"

"If you don't know, sweetheart, be creative. Think where they might be, or all of us are going to be dead."

"Hempstead had an envelope, I saw it. It was on the plant manager's desk. He was using the office."

Track nodded.

The girl shouted, "But we can't go there. His men have gone there."

Track didn't bother answering her, he just kept walking, figuring that if he stopped the leg might not get going again.

They moved along the main floor of the factory, turning a corner past vats of chemicals. Some of them were leaking and they sidestepped the puddles on the concrete floor. The plant manager's office was raised on an island in the center of the main floor. Men were barricaded behind packing crates along the balcony that completely surrounded it. Hiding behind some sort of generator, he could see Zulu and George, trading occasional shots with the remainder of Hempstead's force.

Track drew back behind one of the vats, dragging the woman beside him. "What's in these vats? Anything dangerous?"

"No, not by itself."

"What's this new gas like? Tell me!"

She hesitated and Track slapped her sharply across the face with his hand. Blood trickled from the corner of her mouth and tears welled up in her eyes. "Tell me," he repeated.

"It's less affected by temperature extremes. In fact, temperature doesn't seem to bother it at all."

Track asked her, "What's he going to do with it?"

"I don't know—I don't!"

Track slapped her harder, and she fell to her knees at his feet. "He's had us develop an antidote for this new strain. Anyone who takes it is immune to the effects of the disease that follows when the gas degenerates. And we developed a protective suit that guards against contamination during the gas stage. I don't know what he's planning to do with it. He told Dr. Barnes he was having Herr Gurnheim make one last explosion for him after this. It would ruin the world's economy, and he'd be able to step in as some kind of savior. That's all I know. Please, don't hit me again."

Track only shook his head. He was running out of time and he knew it.

"Where did Gurnheim put the explosives?"

"I didn't know there were any. Please believe me."

Track nodded. He was getting a gut feeling. He looked once at his leg. He wanted to say to hell with

Jilly Mason's sealed orders, but they might be the only way to find the Master, find him and stop him.

Track worked off the safeties on both shotguns. He looked at Sir Abner Chesterton, and Chesterton nodded. Then he looked at Helen Duquesne. "We've got business in the office. You take the stairs to the roof. There's a woman up there with the submachine guns, and she'd shoot you, too. Her name's Desiree. Only girl on the roof with a subgun, so you can't miss her. Tell her who you are and that you're coming with us. And shout it out nice and loud before she shoots you. Then tell her that Dan said get on the chopper's radio and tell the state police to fall back." He looked into the Duquesne woman's eyes. "How big an area would this gas contaminate if the whole factory was blown up?"

"Twenty-five miles—maybe a little more."

Track swallowed hard, then threw his cigar butt to the floor. "They should pull back to thirty miles from the edge of town on all sides. Now get out of here."

And Track dismissed her from his mind. He shouted, "Zulu, George, we're going up, now!" Track dragged his leg after him in a lopsided run, feeling the wetness of new blood as he ran. Gunfire poured down from the balcony surrounding the office.

He kept running, firing both his shotguns, Zulu and George charging the staircase, too, Chesterton's subgun firing. At the base of the stairs, Track emptied both SPASs up the stairwell. Chunks of the packing crates above blew away. The men who had taken shelter there were running toward the office. Chesterton, Zulu, and George emptied their weapons toward them. Track let both riot guns fall to his sides and held the L-Frame in his right fist. He drew the Trapper Scorpion from the Special Weapons rig and thumbed down the ambidextrous safety. He was taking the stairs too slowly. His left leg wouldn't move any faster. There was movement by the office door at the head of the stairs, and Track tucked back. A subgun discharged, and Track felt the heat across his left biceps and shoulder. He fired both pistols, knocking the man back and down, dead.

He was at the top of the stairs now. Blood trickled from his shoulder and the arm was stiffening. Chesterton was beside him, spraying his subgun through the glass into the outer office.

Track half fell, half threw himself against the outer office door, hitting the floor, both pistols firing into the three men who remained. The L-Frame was empty and he fired out the Scorpion. The left side of his ski jacket was wet with his own blood.

One man stood, another was on his knees but gutshot and dying.

From the doorway, subgun and assault-rifle fire hacked into the bodies of the last two security men. As Track lurched past the nearer of them, the man's assault rifle rising to fire, Track hammered the butt of the L-Frame against the man's forehead, then along the bridge of his nose. The head rolled back, the eyes open wide in death.

Track fell against the inner-office door. "Get it," he shouted to Chesterton. Chesterton's subgun blew out the lock. Zulu kicked at the door and it fell inward.

Track stood by sheer willpower now, the entire left side of his body was an ocean of pain and he was drowning in it.

"I have the orders for Mason!" It was Zulu's voice.

Dan Track grinned. "Hey guys—don't let me die or anything or we're all stuck. I'm the only one who can fly the helicopter."

George was beside him now. "I'm carrying you— always did carry you, anyway."

"Bullshit." But Track sagged forward toward his nephew, the taller, younger man catching him up, Track feeling his body go limp over George's shoulder. "The hell with the explosives. Can't stop them wherever they are. Let's—" and he lost it.

DAN TRACK OPENED HIS EYES and saw Desiree's face. "Zulu can try it," she was saying. "He can fly fixed wing."

"Not the same," Track told her. He knew he'd passed out. There were two sets of controls on the Bell, and he shouted, "Zulu—get into the port side seat, hurry!" Track looked at Desiree. "Not dead yet, kid." He turned to George. "Okay show-off. Get me into that pilot's seat before I pass out again. Hurry and don't give me a bumpy ride, son." George drew him up, and Track realized they weren't inside the machine, but still on the snow-packed roof. George half dragged him, half carried him. Track tried to help, but his body was not responding. Chesterton was beside him, his right arm bloodied. He didn't remember Chesterton being wounded.

He was being carried now—Desiree had his feet, George his upper body. "You guys are great," Track observed. "Get me strapped in there."

He was losing it again. He bit his tongue and his eyes opened wider for an instant.

Suddenly, he was in the pilot's seat but he didn't remember getting there. Desiree had her hands in his pockets. "That tickles, kid. Looking for the key?"

"I've got it."

Track took it from her, missed the keyhole the first time, made it the second.

"All right, Zulu, watch me. If I pass out, get me awake enough to tell you what to do."

"Of course, Major. Rest assured."

Track started working the controls, powering up. The main rotor was turning but not fast enough. He told himself that. Not fast enough. His eyes were closing. He opened them—had he been unconscious? Blacked out? The rotors were turning now, both of them, the rhythm sounding right. He couldn't see the controls that well. Too much blood loss, he told himself. "Strap in, dammit!" He took the machine up, and the helicopter lurched wildly to starboard, Track recovered, and the machine lurched wildly to port. Overcompensating, he told himself. He was very tired of it all.

He consciously watched his hand on the stick. The machine was coming under control, still rising as he glanced beneath them. He fixed that, turning the chopper a full 180, degrees then throttling out for speed. "Hang on, gang!" He couldn't handle it—but he had to handle it.

He tried looking for the airspeed indicator, and couldn't remember where it was. He lurched forward and the machine started to dive. But Desiree was kneeling behind him and pulled him up. He had control again. "So this is how it feels when you bleed to death. Son of a bitch," he told her. It was like being high.

He heard a roar behind them and he twisted in his seat and look back. A giant fireball was rising where a moment earlier the factory had been. "Aw shit," he snarled, pouring on the airspeed now.

It was a simple thing, he told himself. Outrun the gas cloud and land the machine. If he didn't, they would all die. He started telling himself, "Don't lose it. Don't... lose... it... don't... don't... lose it."

Everything was a blur to him and he realized that consciousness was something he was falling out of and then back into. Once his eyes closed.

When he opened them somehow—the machine had landed and Zulu was shouting, ''Major, you are miraculous, sir!'' And Desiree was crying and kissing him at the same time. Chesterton was looking on, smiling. And George was white as a ghost.

33

He never did understand how he had gotten the helicopter to land.

And Jilly Mason's sealed orders had proven to be a useless dead end.

A week in the hospital, three of the days spent in therapy for his leg, then another week of daily visits to the hospital for additional therapy and he was well enough to attend George's wedding to Ellen. He didn't dance the night away with Desiree at the reception, but he managed two slow dances with her and did a lot of sitting. He did a substantial but not exorbitant amount of drinking with George's father, Robert, Sir Abner Chesterton and Zulu. Several times Desiree gave him worried looks.

Ellen, Track had told George when they had shaken hands that last time, was a beautiful bride. And Track had shrugged his shoulders and thrown his arms around his nephew, the younger man who in so many ways had been and always would be like a son to him.

The day following the wedding, Track plunged himself into a different sort of task. He worked with teams of computer experts, scientists who were analyzing data on the Master's new gas provided by the now highly cooperative Helen Duquesne, and he joined in conferences with high-ranking military and police officials from countries around the world.

The face of the Master of D.E.A.T.H. adorned post offices, newspapers and televisions everywhere. But still, it seemed sometimes to Track, the Earth had opened up and swallowed the man. Five weeks had passed since the demolition of the factory where the gas had been produced. No innocent lives had been claimed and the city of Idatana had found itself setting records for overall community good health. A curious side effect of the gas, it seemed, was that it destroyed many of the common causes of viral infections. There was some talk among the scientists with whom Track conferred that further research into the Master's lethal gas might someday lead to the development of a throat spray that would render the user immune to several of the more common and bothersome strains of flu viruses.

At the end of the fifth week, Sir Abner Chesterton had volunteered to buy dinner at the Tavern On the Green on the fringe of New York's Central Park. Track, Desiree and Zulu had promptly accepted.

It was one of his favorite places to eat in the world.

It was a pleasant night as they left the restaurant, its lights twinkling like something out of a child's fairy story behind them. Desiree suggested, "Why don't we go for a walk? We can come back here and catch a taxi."

Chesterton said, "But my dear, this is Central Park."

Zulu observed. "But there are four of us. Major Track is invariably armed and you are armed, Sir Abner. I am, of course, armed."

"I've got mine," Desiree smiled, patting the black beaded bag she held clutched in her hand. "Come on, it's so nice out."

Track exhaled a long sigh. "Okay, a little walk," and he took Desiree's arm in his as they started into the park.

Track was aware of the night's sounds: a bird calling somewhere in the darkness, the barking of a dog, the clicking of Desiree's black high heels on the pavement beside him, the muted voices of Chesterton and Zulu discussing English football.

No mention of the Master of D.E.A.T.H. had been made throughout the evening though he was their constant topic of conversation throughout the day.

Track remembered something Baslovitch had told him about a conversation he'd had with George, when "Peter" and "Louise" had paid him a surprise visit at the hospital in Seattle. Baslovitch had told George the very fact that he and Tatiana might meet their demise at any time heightened living and awareness.

Track had felt that in these past weeks. For at any moment, the Master might unleash his gas, as yet, scientists working around the clock had not developed a defense. Helen Duquesne had known nothing of the antidote for the disease the gas imparted—it had been a project of the Master's chief scientist, Dr. Barnes. And none except Barnes and the Master, who had personally assisted Barnes in its development, were privy to its secret.

It was this threat of death that heightened his enjoyment of life. The world at large knew nothing of the Master's intent. And the secrecy of the knowledge Track and the relative few involved in combating the threat shared, only enhanced his awareness each day.

Desiree was talking to him. "Things are working out for George and Ellen. She's so sweet."

"I'm sorry," he said as he smiled, looking at her, holding her arm more closely. "I wasn't listening."

"What are you thinking about?" She smiled back.

"Oh, I don't know. That thing Sergei told me, about life being sweeter because it was so fragile—stuff like that." He laughed. "Dan Track's *Thoughts on the*

Meaning of Life. That's right friends, this amazing book can be yours for the incredibly low, low price of $9.95 And, if you act now, at no extra cost, we'll include a free book of matches so you can burn the book and never risk reading it again. And—''

"Oh, shut up," she said with a laugh.

He folded his arm around her as they walked deeper into the park. He started to chuckle.

"What are you laughing about now?"

"I was just thinking," and he raised his voice. "Hey, Sir Abner, Zulu? I was just thinking. If some gang of muggers comes after us, boy are they in for a shock, huh?"

He looked back. Chesterton was laughing, even Zulu smiled. And Track made a funny voice and said, "Hey, mother. Gimme your wallet, huh, or I'll cut ya!" And he dropped his voice and stuck out his right hand with an imaginary gun in it. "Yeah fool, come on, cut me— bang!"

But then another voice cut across his—this one from the darkness. "Freeze!" There was a burst of silenced subgun fire; Track knew the sound well. He pushed Desiree behind him, his hand darting under his jacket for the Trapper Scorpion. The voice again. "We're here from the Master—eight of us with automatic weapons. Move and you're dead."

The gun was in Track's hand, but he didn't raise it. In the cone of light from a streetlamp, figures appeared, ringing them. Uzi machine guns were in their hands.

Sir Abner Chesterton cleared his throat and Zulu remarked, "If Mohammed cannot come to the mountain, then the mountain shall come to Mohammed."

Track didn't say anything.

SUBGUNS TRAINED ON THEM UNWAVERINGLY, they had been transported in two vans, Track and Desiree in one, Zulu and Chesterton in the second. Their initial destination was an airfield in upstate New York. Their weapons taken, the four were locked into the passenger compartment of an unmarked business jet, a quartet of men with submachine guns watching them, saying nothing.

Desiree had fallen asleep in Track's arms, finally, but Track had not allowed himself the luxury of sleep. They landed once for refueling, then were airborne again, Track unable to see where they were when they landed, nor monitor their journey at all because the porthole curtains were drawn. When he had tried to raise one, one of the silent, subgun-armed guards had brandished his weapon.

There was the old movie ploy: "You wouldn't fire that in here. We could depressurize." But since he had no idea what type of 9mm ammo was being used in the Uzis and since sudden cabin depressurization would have killed him, Desiree, Sir Abner and Zulu, as well as the four guards, he passed on the old line.

After four hours of flight following the refueling stop, the aircraft landed once again.

There was a period of frustrating inactivity. Desiree was awake now, and he envied her common sense. His eyes burned from the lack of sleep.

The door opened and Track turned to look toward it. A tall, good-looking, athletic sort of man with a warm smile and dead eyes entered the aircraft. "Together at last," the man enthused, his voice carrying a slight British accent. "I am the Master." Track raised his right hand and waved.

THE SUNLIGHT was brilliant as they walked across the airfield, the Master at their center. The air was warm, breezy—balmy. Track removed his suit coat and hooked it over his shoulder with his thumb.

"I hope the journey wasn't too unpleasant," the Master said, looking at them one at a time, then turning to look ahead.

"Why did you bring us here?"

Desiree asked the question, and like Track was removing her jacket. Track helped her, the short black jacket gone, her bare arms revealed.

The Master turned to her and smiled. "All of you seemed so intent on us getting together. Well, I felt somehow socially obligated to help."

"Tell me, sir," Zulu began, "is it your intention to simply bore us to death with your company, or do you have other plans for our respective ends?"

"Very good, Zulu—very good. And please, forgive my familiarity. But I feel somehow intimate with all of you. As to your question, no, I shall not bore you to death. In fact, your deaths are not in my immediate plans at all. All of you might live to ripe old ages. No, had I wished your deaths, there might have been many times since the affair in Idatana."

They stopped before a brick structure built at the base of a huge mound. The door of the structure appeared to be made of high-strength steel. Around the airfield they had seen numerous khaki-clad, helmeted men with submachine guns. Two more stood flanking the door.

The Master nodded and one of them caused the steel door to slide away and disappear. "Shall we?" The Master stepped aside for Desiree to enter ahead of him, and allowed Track to walk beside her. From behind him now, Track heard the Master's voice. "Don't attempt to cause me physical harm. My guards are everywhere and you most assuredly would die."

They were in a small, winding corridor, the floor angling steeply downward. "Tell me," Track asked over his shoulder, trying to keep an edge from his voice. "Is this your global headquarters for world domination?"

The Master laughed. "I'm pleased you are retaining your sense of humor, Dan. And may I say, you and Desiree make a lovely couple."

"Thank you," Desiree said curtly.

"Through that second door on your right, if you please."

More guards on each of the doors, Track with Desiree beside him stopping before the second door on the right.

The guard opened the door and the Master urged, "Please, go in."

Track stepped through ahead of Desiree into a massive conference room. The high walls curved in at the top and were capped with a dome. The walls were adorned with maps. At the center of the room was a long conference table. "I'm sorry, this place is a liitle formal," the Master said. "Why don't we arrange ourselves about this table and chat."

Track looked at Desiree and she winked. He smiled at her and helped her into one of the seats on the near side of the table, then settled into the chair beside her, folding his sportcoat over his knee.

He felt mildly ridiculous. The Special Weapons shoulder rig was empty of a gun.

Chesterton and Zulu sat on the opposite side of the table from them.

The Master sat at the conference table's head. Another uniformed guard appeared from the far end of the room, but instead of a submachine gun, he carried a tray. "I hope you all like pineapple juice. It's fresh. They grow here on the island in great abundance."

"Where are we, if you don't mind my asking?" Chesterton asked.

"Certainly. Forgive my rudeness. We're on a small island off Barbados. A halcyon spot—for lovers especially so," and he bowed his head toward Track and Desiree. "I would have had George and Ellen join us, but I decided against it. The travel might have been fatiguing to someone in a wheelchair."

Track leaned across the table, "You touch either of them, and I'll come back from the grave and kill you if I have to."

The Master shook his head, frowning. "Really, but they are well, as far as I know. I haven't molested them—rest assured," and he poured from the pitcher filling five glasses and setting them at the center of the table, still on the tray. The unarmed man in the guard's uniform disappeared. They were alone in the room with the Master of D.E.A.T.H.

"Please, do you think it's poisoned or drugged or something?" And he gestured toward the five glasses, taking one, downing half of its contents. "There—safe. I merely find it a satisfying pick-me-up."

"Where's Dr. Barnes?" Track asked.

"Oh my, Helen Duquesne has been talking, hasn't she?" the Master said. "Dr. Barnes had become bothered by his conscience, and once the new strain of gas had been developed, well—his conscience will never bother him again."

"What time, may I ask, is shuffleboard scheduled?" Zulu said with a smile.

"Very good. How droll you are, sir." The Master smiled back.

Track shrugged and took a glass of the juice, sniffing at it, then taking a sip.

"You are now poisoned! I have drunk the antidote previously!" And the Master hammered his fist on the table and laughed like a hyena. "I too can make jokes, as you see!"

Track took another sip of his juice. "What do you want?"

"I merely desired your company and your safety. In less than an hour," the Master said, gazing at his watch, "Herr Gurnheim will assist me in the manipulation of a certain button—"

"It takes two of you to push a button?" Track asked, but didn't wait for an answer. "Sir Abner, give me a cigarette please. It's a little too confined in here for a cigar."

"Quite," and Chesterton handed over his cigarette case. Track lit one with his own lighter and slid the cigarette case back across the table. A spotless ashtray was before each seat at the table. Track baptized one, molding a tip on the cigarette as he exhaled.

"I was saying," the Master continued, "in less than an hour, Herr Gurnheim and I shall push a button. The button will send a radio signal to a satellite I own—a perfectly harmless, perfectly ordinary communications satellite," and he nodded differentially to Dan Track. "I know your fondness for space weapons, Dan. The satellite will broadcast a signal to five hundred different transmitters located throughout the United States, Canada and Europe. The transmitters will activate five hundred explosive charges. I consider it a marvellous pyrotechnic display because of its precision, though I'll confess Klaus Gurnheim was disappointed because the explosions in and of themselves will be terribly spectacular. But—" he smiled again "—each tiny explosion will rupture a drum containing a satisfactorily large quantity of my little gas. Each city will be poisoned. Millions will die. There will be utter chaos. Soon, the disease will take over. Millions more will die. And then, in my benevolence, I shall step forward, with limited but adequate quantities of the antidote for the bacterial effect. Millions of lives will be saved. I shall be seen as a great savior, a great humanitarian. Of course—'' he spread his palms outward ''—the antidote is very costly. Great sums of money will be needed to procure it. And I am the only source. I shall strip the cost to the bone, of course. I estimate that I will control forty percent of the world's wealth. I will rule.''

''No offense, dear boy,'' Chesterton said, smiling broadly, ''but you are quite insane.''

The Master smiled. ''I have brought the four of you here and conspicuously not brought George and Ellen and George's father, Robert. I offer the four of you here, and the three not present with whom you have emotional attachment, the chance to live. There will be chaos after the button is pushed. I will require persons with a sense of justice and law, persons basically good in nature, to administer under me such a world—or otherwise the chaos will never cease. I offer life to you four and life for the three others, in exchange for loyalty. Out of what you would interpret as evil, can come great good. And there you have it. Personal wealth, of course. Personal power. But more importantly, you could reshape the world.''

Track looked at the Master of D.E.A.T.H. He asked the question with sincerity. ''Are you the devil?''

The Master of D.E.A.T.H. only laughed. ''I shall leave you to decide. Feel free to walk about the complex. Feel free to talk with Herr Gurnheim. I am confident you will make the sensible decision. My guards are everywhere, so be confident of your safety.'' The Master rose, smiled, checked his watch and started to walk from the room.

Dan Track looked from Desiree to Zulu to Sir Abner Chesterton.

The decision had been made. There never really was any decision to make.

Track pushed back the chair and ran, hurling his body against the body of the Master of D.E.A.T.H., bulldogging him to the carpeted floor, the first two fingers of Track's left hand hooking into the Master's nostrils, snapping the head back, the Master screaming. Track's right hand grasped the Master's throat, his fist closing in a death grip over the larynx as he snapped the head all the way back. He heard bone crack and break as his fingers crushed the voice box.

The Master of D.E.A.T.H. was dead.

Dan Track climbed to his feet, his hands shaking. Desiree was beside him, his coat hugged in her arms. "So much for surrendering to temptation." She smiled, leaning up and kissing him.

He looked at the dead body of the Master. But he wondered if he had surrendered. Had the temptation been the killing?

He took his coat, pulling it on. "The Master said we could take a walk, let's do it. We'll nail the first guard we see and get his gun. We'll find Gurnheim, dismantle his equipment if we live that long, then fight our way back to the plane. Our own guns must be on board. And if we can get Gurnheim out, he can pinpoint the locations of the gas canisters for us."

He stuck out his right hand and Chesterton took it. Zulu closed his hand over theirs, and Desiree placed hers atop the other three.

Dan Track felt himself smiling. He started for the door and turned the knob.

The guard outside scarcely looked at him.

Track walked past him and Desiree stopped in front of him. "The Master said we could look around. I need a ladies' room."

"There's one—" he started, gesturing down the corridor. Suddenly, Zulu's hand closed over his throat, lifting the man bodily. Zulu thrust the man upward, smashing the helmet and the head beneath it against the low ceiling as Desiree's hands closed over the subgun.

Zulu threw the body through the open door and Chesterton closed it.

Track took the Uzi, shrugging out of his coat again, covering the subgun with it.

He jerked his head down the corridor, asking Desiree, "You really need a ladies' room? I mean, we can wait."

"I went on the plane," she said.

As they walked on, the hallway split into two corridors; a guard with a submachine gun stood where the two new passageways met. Track smiled at him. "Excuse me, but which is the way to Herr Gurnheim's facility? We haven't seen him in some time. The Master said it was all right."

The guard gestured down the corridor to the left. Somehow Track had thought it would be that way.

He smiled to the guard and said, "Thanks," and started past him.

Track closed his eyes as Desiree asked, "Pardon me, I need a ladies' room. Is there—"

"Yes ma'am, back up the corridor and—aagh!" Track looked around. Zulu's left hand covered the man's mouth, while his right hand closed over the face. The head slammed back against the concrete wall of the corridor. Zulu let the body fall as Desiree grabbed the subgun. Chesterton took off his blazer, taking the subgun and folding the jacket over it.

Track gestured down the corridor and they kept walking, the corridor angling downward, curving to the left. Ahead were two guards. Under his breath, he murmured to Desiree beside him, "Don't try the ladies' room dodge again."

"You ask for a men's room then, I don't care."

The guards flanked another bombproof door and Track assumed it was Gurnheim's location.

Chesterton suddenly walked past him, right up to the two guards. Track slowed his pace a little. Chesterton's coat dropped and the Uzi fired a 3-round burst into each guard, the men's bodies slamming back against the corridor wall.

Desiree ran forward, picking up Chesterton's coat, then one of the Uzi's. Zulu took the second. None of the guards so far had carried spare magazines.

As Track pulled on his jacket, Chesterton said almost apologetically, "I thought the direct approach might be best."

Zulu's hand was already on the handle of the bombproof door, sliding the door away as Track worked back the bolt on his Uzi. Track stormed through into a room half the size of the conference room. Two more armed guards confronted him and Track sprayed the Uzi toward them. There were the sounds of shattering glass, a scream and a burst of subgun fire ripped into the ceiling as one of the guards triggered his weapon.

Standing at the approximate center of the room, his hands poised over a control panel, Track saw Klaus Gurnheim. "Gurnheim!"

An alarm was sounding throughout the complex now, a high shrieking whistle.

"Take the door," Track shouted behind him, starting across the room.

Gurnheim called out to him, "One step closer and I shall push the button, herr Major!"

Track stopped.

When the Master had mentioned that he and Gurnheim would push the button, he had also consulted his wristwatch. Dan Track gambled then, with millions of lives. "The satellite isn't in position yet, Gurnheim, it won't be for forty-five minutes or so. You're bluffing.

If you push that button, I'll beat you to death with my bare hands—just for fun. If you don't, you've got a ticket out of here.''

"To prison!"

"Yeah." Track nodded. "It beats the alternative, though, doesn't it?"

Klaus Gurnheim turned away from the console. "You are right. To push the button now would do no good."

Track walked toward the man and stopped less than a yard from him. "Dismantle the radio equipment—so it can't be used."

"Yes," Gurnheim answered, his shoulders slumped. "Zulu, help him!"

Track started back toward the door as Zulu ran from it. Track glanced back once. Gurnheim was on his knees beside the console a screwdriver in his hand.

Track stopped at the door. No guards rushed them, yet. The whistlelike siren still wailed. "Sir Abner, if Gurnheim has explosives stored here, you and Zulu take him with you and have him set them to blow. Desiree and I are going up the corridor to get to the plane and get it started." He turned to look for Desiree. She was working her way around the room, scooping up documents in her arms.

Chesterton handed Track a second Uzi. "You might need this, Zulu has two. Makes three for each team."

Track nodded. Then he shouted back to Gurnheim, still working beneath the console. "How much longer, Gurnheim?"

"Perhaps a minutes, perhaps two. I am removing the modulator so that the frequency cannot be adjusted. It will be useless."

"You have explosives here?"

Gurnheim didn't answer.

Track shouted to him again.

This time Gurnheim answered. "Yes, stored along this corridor, herr Major!"

"You go with Zulu and Sir Abner. Set the explosives to blow!"

"But there is enough to destroy the entire complex!"

"I was hoping you'd say that." And Track shouted to Zulu, "Give yourselves enough time to get back outside to the field. Hurry! We'll be waiting."

"Of course," and Zulu's head ducked back beneath the console beside Gurnheim.

"Good luck," Track told Chesterton. Desiree was beside him again.

"I have everything I can carry."

Track nodded, grabbing some of the documents from her, stuffing them into his pockets: charts, graphs, chemical formulas. Somewhere among them, he hoped, would be the formula for the new gas so it could be neutralized.

He started into the corridor, cautioning, "Stay close, kid." He held a Uzi in each fist.

The wailing of the sirens grew louder as he climbed the sloping hallway, quickening his pace.

Subgun fire tore into the plaster and he tucked back, keeping Desiree behind him, firing both weapons in answer. There was more enemy fire as uniformed guards packed the end of the corridor.

He pushed Desiree farther back, into an open doorway as subgun fire ripped into the wall near his head. He shouted over it. "Listen! Listen!"

The gunfire ceased.

"Gurnheim is wiring this place to blow right now. Stick around shooting at us and all any of you'll be is dead!"

Track waited, then edged forward from the protection of the doorway. The guards were running, but toward the outside.

Track started running, too, now, Desiree beside him. He had lost track of the number of minutes it had been since he'd ordered Gurnheim to wire the facility to blow.

As he reached the junction of the two corridors a pair of guards raised their weapons to fire. Track fired both Uzi's and the guards went down.

Track dropped to his knees beside them wrenching the magazines from their weapons, thrusting the two spares into his belt. "Let's go," and he urged Desiree ahead, running behind her. The sirens were louder still.

The door from the Master's conference room opened, a guard framing himself in the opening. Track threw Desiree down and went into a roll. Coming up, he fired as the guard's weapon fired, both Uzi's in Track's fists emptying into the guard.

Desiree was up and running, clinging to the sheaves of paper she carried.

As Track ran, he switched to the fresh magazines for his weapon. The outside was very near now—he could smell the fresher air, feel the rise in temperature.

Outdoors, guards were running everywhere and the airfield on which they had landed was alive with vehicles going in all directions, planes trying to take off. Panic.

Two men were boarding a Jeep and Track fired on them both, cutting them down. He ran for the vehicle, Desiree at his side. Sliding behind the wheel, he fired the ignition. "Hang on," he shouted, throwing the vehicle into gear. Men were scrambling aboard the business jet that had transported them to the island—it was the only plane on the field big enough for the four of them and Gurnheim. Track aimed the Jeep toward it, accelerating, racing through the gears, cutting the wheel as he angled toward the aircraft.

Someone was starting one of the engines.

"Damn." The windshield of the Jeep was turned down, the wind lashing at his face and hair. A man beside the jet turned to fire his weapon and Track thrust one of the Uzi's across the dash and fired, cutting the guard down with a burst into the chest.

Track threw down the Uzi, fighting the steering wheel and downshifting, skidding the Jeep to a halt less than ten yards from the aircraft.

Catching up the both subguns, he jumped from the Jeep and ran toward the jet. A face appeared in the door. Track fired into it and a body tumbled down the folding steps.

Track jumped the dead man and took the steps three at a time, ducking his head, throwing himself through the open doorway. Two men stood with Uzi's at the forward section of the fuselage, and Track fired out both weapons in his hands. Nine-millimetre targets stung into the seat beside his head.

Both men went down.

Track looked to the doorway and saw Desiree, her arms still laden with the documents, rush into the cabin.

She threw the papers on the floor of the aircraft and tossed Track her subgun.

He caught it, starting forward along the fuselage. The door to the pilot's cabin opened and Track recognized their pilot. The man held a pistol in his right fist. Track shot him in the throat, the body rocking back.

He glanced back to Desiree and saw her picking up the weapons from the two fallen guards. He strode into the pilot's cabin and settled behind the controls.

"I see them! Zulu and Sir Abner—they have Gurnheim!" Desiree shouted.

He looked through the cockpit window. Vehicles were everywhere, crisscrossing the field. Then Track saw them in a pickup truck—Chesterton and Gurnheim were in the bed, Chesterton's subgun firing.

Track started the preflight check again. "Desiree, there should be wheel chocks out there. Have Zulu see to them!"

"Right!"

The fuel gauge registered well over half. He had no idea what the consumption rate was for the craft, but it would be enough to get them someplace.

The pickup truck with Chesterton, Zulu and Gurnheim skidded to a halt and he could hear Desiree yelling to Zulu, saw Zulu disappear beneath the fuselage for a moment.

He heard Chesterton shouting, "The explosives should blow in less than two minutes!"

"It will destroy the field, as well. We'll all be—" Gurnheim's frightened voice added.

"Shut Gurnheim up," Track snarled over his shoulder.

He saw Zulu again, waving an "all clear."

Track started throttling up, taxiing ahead, glancing back once. Zulu was climbing aboard.

Trucks and jeeps were everywhere, and as Track turned the craft into the wind, it was impossible to tell if he would have sufficient take-off distance. "Get that door secured—and strap in, guys!"

Track moved the aircraft ahead, his speed increasing steadily.

A pickup truck swerved to avoid him. And off to his side a single-engine plane was trying to take off ahead of him. A Jeep slammed into it and both machines were consumed in a ball of flame. Track increased his speed, angling the craft to starboard, cutting across the runway at a slight diagonal now. The end of the field was coming up fast and a corrugated metal building sat just beyond. "Aww shit," he murmured.

Track throttled out both engines as Desiree lurched into the copilot's seat beside him.

"If we don't make it—well, we don't make it to-gether," she said with a smile.

Track glanced at her, then gave the twin-engine jet everything it had, his hand finding the landing-gear switch as they cleared the building. He'd hunched his shoulders against the impact, but there was none.

As the aircraft climbed, he settled back into his seat and looked out his side window. Explosions were ripping across the mound that formed the entrance to the underground complex, chunks of the field flying skyward, flames spreading as vehicles and aircraft were engulfed.

He reached out and squeezed Desiree's hand as he started the aircraft banking to port to circle over the field and head out to sea. And Dan Track called over his shoulder. "Gurnheim, you're a rotten guy, but when you blow something up...what can I say!"

MORE GREAT ACTION
COMING SOON

When there's no one else to turn to!

#10 Cocaine Run
by Jerry Ahern

The cocaine-for-guns trading racket seizes another victim when the daughter of a prominent U.S. senator becomes a willing accomplice in a deadly game. When Track is asked to rescue her, he decides to play a lone hand and flies to the headquarters of the drug trade in Central America. Against a background of terrorism and revolution, Track is drawn further into the rat-infested sewers of the drug world, until the hunter becomes the hunted.

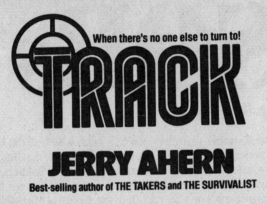

**Nile Barrabas and the
Soldiers of Barrabas are the**

by Jack Hild

Nile Barrabas is a nervy son of a bitch who was the last
American soldier out of Vietnam and the first man into a
new kind of action. His warriors, called the Soldiers of
Barrabas, have one very simple ambition: to do what the
Marines can't or won't do. Join the Barrabas blitz! Each
book hits new heights—this is brawling at its best!

"Nile Barrabas is one tough SOB himself.... A wealth of
detail.... SOBs does the job!"
—*West Coast Review of Books*

#1 The Barrabas Run   #6 Red Hammer Down
#2 The Plains of Fire   #7 River of Flesh
#3 Butchers of Eden   #8 Eye of the Fire
#4 Show No Mercy   #9 Some Choose Hell
#5 Gulag War

GET THE NEW WAR BOOK AND MACK BOLAN BUMPER STICKER FREE!

Mail this coupon today!